MW01145673

Shores of the Marrow

The Haunted Series
Book 6
Patrick Logan

Books by Patrick Logan

The Haunted Series

Book 1: Shallow Graves

Book 2: The Seventh Ward

Book 3: Seaforth Prison

Book 4: Scarsdale Crematorium

Book 5: Sacred Heart Orphanage

Book 6: Shores of the Marrow

Insatiable Series

Book 1: Skin

Book 2: Crackers

Book 3: Flesh

Book 4: Parasite

Book 4.5: Knuckles

Book 5: Stitches

Family Values Trilogy

Witch (Prequel)

Mother

Father

Daughter

This book is a work of fiction. Names, characters, places, and incidents in this book are either entirely imaginary or are used fictitiously. Any resemblance to actual people, living or dead, or of places, events, or locales is entirely coincidental.

Copyright © Patrick Logan 2017
Cover design: Ebook Launch (www.ebooklaunch.com)
Interior design: © Patrick Logan 2017

All rights reserved.

This book, or parts thereof, cannot be reproduced, scanned, or disseminated in any print or electronic form.

Third Edition: March 2018

Prologue

"NO! WE CAN'T LEAVE her! *No!*" Robert screamed at the top of his lungs. "*Nooooo!*"

But the arms that pulled him back were too powerful, too strong, and before he knew it, he was being shoved into a small, dimly-lit room, and then up a ladder. Visions of Bella, staring at him with her dark eyes jutting out from behind her strange haircut, the blade against Shelly's soft white skin, filled his mind.

They have her... and they have my baby.

The thought, the realization, was like an icepick striking him directly in the center of his forehead.

Unseen hands forced him onward, shoving him upward, into some sort of air vent, but these facts barely registered with Robert. Instead, his fractured mind was replaying a series of images—Bella's smiling face, the fear plastered on Shelly's—in something akin to stop-motion animation.

He saw his father, Leland Black, The Goat, and he watched as the winged-beast extricated itself from the gaping hole in the center of Sean Sommer's chest as if undergoing some sort of bastardized birth.

He's here... Carson finally brought Leland back from the Marrow. The Goat was here.

"No!" Robert screamed again, but this time a filthy hand wrapped around his mouth, muffling him.

"Keep moving," Agent Cherry ordered, shoving him even harder.

He had been in this vent once before, a part of his mind realized, only back then it hadn't been a drunk FBI Agent pushing him through, but a much younger Sean Sommers.

Sean... the man who had brought him back into the fold on that deadly, rainy night. The man who couldn't just leave him alone, couldn't let him live a normal life. Sean, who was dead now; his quiddity sucked from him by his mother, the tattered vessel that had once held the ancient man ripped apart by his father.

Tears streamed down his face, and Robert couldn't help but think that *everything* was gone, stolen from him.

Destroyed.

First Amy and Wendy, then Shelly and his unborn child. Everything ripped from his grasp.

His life, his mind, his sanity.

Somewhere far away, Robert felt his body being lowered down a ladder and into a small room. The air around him still thrummed with that horrible electrical energy, and there was a slight tremble to the earth, but Robert couldn't tell if this was just his body shaking or if the ground itself was moving.

"In here," a gruff voice instructed, and a large air filter was peeled away from the wall, revealing a dark tunnel cut into the stone.

Robert hesitated as he stared into that tunnel of dirt. The musty smell of moist earth invaded his nostrils, and he was reminded of the briny, acidic scent of the sea, of his short time at Seaforth Prison.

You must stay in control, a voice inside his head suddenly chimed. *You have to keep it together.*

It was Helen.

Robert, for both our sake's, and for the sake of Shelly and your child, you can't let the darkness take over.

But despite the plea, Robert felt his vision narrowing.

A hand landed gently on his shoulder, momentarily bringing him back from the brink.

He turned and stared into the cloak that his mother used to cover herself. Even though Robert couldn't see her eyes, he knew that she was looking at him.

Into him.

"Robert, please," was all she said.

Summoning the last of his will, Robert stepped into the tunnel and started to run.

The others followed.

***

The tunnel opened on the side of a hill overlooking Sacred Heart Orphanage. As Robert stared at the building below, light continued to spill from each of the dozens of windows, and a great beam of it shot from the roof, extending upward into a roiling sky.

There were seven of them on that hill, their dirt-smeared faces staring down in abject horror: there was Robert, Cal, Agent Cherry, the Cloak, and the younger of the two detectives, Hugh. There was also Aiden, who had made the trek up the hill to join them.

His body had acquired more texture, and Robert realized that he was no longer able to see through the man as he once had.

Something wrong was happening here, something terrible.

And there was nothing any of them could do to stop it.

The Goat is here…

Wind drifted up the slope, sending their grimy hair swirling about their dirt-smeared faces.

No one said anything for what felt like ages.

Eventually, it was Hugh who spoke.

"What was that?" he whispered.

The only answer came from the sky itself: it frothed madly, clouds crawling over one another like cicadas trapped in a mason jar. For an instant, Robert thought that the heavens themselves would tear open and that quiddity would spill forth, filling this world with their madness, with their evil.

But just as the cloud dance reached a fever pitch, the light blinked out, and their illumination was reduced to the bluish cast of a crescent moon.

The Cloak pushed the heavy hood off her head, revealing her scarred face.

Robert was drawn to his mother's good eye.

Chloe's appearance was perhaps even more horrifying than the creature that he had seen climb out of the Marrow, but he wasn't disgusted.

Instead, he felt a pang of sadness deep in the pit of his stomach.

He wasn't the only one who had lost during this battle.

And some of them had suffered for much longer than he had.

Chloe had two sons, two boys who had been drawn to opposite sides of this battle between good and evil, between what was right and what was decidedly evil.

Trapped in the strange, mystical sea between life and death.

With a shuddering sigh, Robert tore his eyes from his mother's scarred face and looked to Cal, who was staring down at the Orphanage, his cheeks wet with tears. Then he glanced at Hugh, who looked equally as confused as frightened, and then to Agent Cherry. The man's blond hair was damp with sweat, his mouth a thin line.

Aiden was similarly stone-faced, but his eyes... there was a darkness to his eyes that made Robert tremble.

Yes, they had all lost something in this battle.

A horrible growl, a deep rumbling sound that rattled molars and blurred vision, filled the night, seeming to somehow *become* it. It was a sound that Robert knew could only have been made by one entity, and he felt his entire body go numb.

On the heels of this howl, Chloe Black finally spoke up, her gravelly voice torn from her throat by the wind.

"We need to move... it isn't safe here. We still have work to do. This... this is only the beginning."

Part I – The Scent of the Marrow

Chapter 1

TWENTY-FIVE YEARS AGO

Callum Godfrey pulled his jeans up and then sucked in his gut before doing up the button. When he relaxed, his stomach flopped over the waistband, and the hard material cut into his skin. He teased his white t-shirt down, tucking it into the front first, and then turning sideways to look at himself in the full-length mirror on the back of his door.

He grimaced at the sight, then pulled it back out again, letting it hang loosely.

Much better, he thought.

"Cal, get downstairs and eat your breakfast! You're going to be late for school!"

Cal took one more look at himself in the mirror, smoothed his dark hair, which immediately sprung back to near exactly the way it had been, then opened the door to his bedroom.

"Coming!" he shouted, taking the stairs two at a time. He reached the landing and saw his mom standing there, lunch bag in hand. "Thanks," he said, as he grabbed it.

"What about breakfast?" his father hollered from the kitchen.

Cal looked over his shoulder to the kitchen. David Godfrey, dressed in his usual crisp white dress shirt and blue slacks, stared back overtop of his glasses that were pulled down onto the bridge of his nose.

"Not hungry," Cal said simply. His father's eyes moved to Cal's shirt, which was untucked, and therefore against the school dress code, so quickly that he didn't think that Cal noticed.

But Cal noticed.

"Not hungry," he repeated, trying not to frown.

"Okay, son. Have a good day at school."

Cal nodded and turned to his mom. She leaned down and he gave her a quick peck on the cheek, and he rolled his eyes.

"Bye, mom."

Cal hurried from the house just in time to see the yellow school bus pull away from the curb. For appearances, he chased after it, but his effort was manufactured at best. When he turned the corner, and out of sight of his mother who he knew had been watching from the front door of their house, he stopped, and then glanced around for his friends.

On cue, two boys and a girl came into view, beaming smiles plastered on their faces.

"Cally-boy!" the taller of the two boys shouted, raising his hand up high. Cal slapped him with a high-five, then did the same with the other boy.

"Hey Brent, Hank."

The girl also raised her hand, but when Cal went to high-five her, he took some mustard off the slap, and this somehow served to make it a less coordinated movement.

Instead of hearing the satisfying *smack* of palm on palm, Cal missed her much smaller hand and thudded against her shoulder instead. Cal started to blush immediately.

"Heh, sorry," he grumbled. "'Sup Stacey."

Stacey smiled broadly.

"Hey, Cal. Missed the bus again today?"

Cal chuckled.

Accidentally on purpose.

Hank, who was taller than all of them by nearly a foot, but whom Cal still had at least forty pounds on, looked around nervously before pulling a pack of cigarettes from his pocket.

"Who wants one?" he asked, teasing one out for himself.

Stacey shook her head, but Brent was eager. He tossed his head to the side, forcing his shaggy blond hair from his face, and grabbed one.

Hank raised his eyes to Cal's.

"How 'bout you?" he asked, holding the pack out.

Cal scanned Hank's dark eyes buried behind thick spectacles, then Brent's, and finally Stacey's.

"No... no, I'm all right. Mrs. Johnson is a hawk for that shit. Last week, she said that Tom Tricker smelled of smoke and sent him right to the office. He said that it had been two days since he had a cigarette, and even then, it had only been a drag or two."

Brent shook his head.

"It wasn't two days since he had a smoke, it was early that morning; I know, because it was my smoke."

Cal shrugged.

"Whatever, but I don't want her calling my mom again. She'll have a shit."

"Doesn't matter, cuz we ain't even going to school today, are we, guys?" Hank said with a grin.

He moved the pack even closer to Cal.

Not going today?

Cal's thoughts turned to his mother, to the brown lunch bag that she had given him, which he still clutched in a suddenly sweaty hand.

"Nope, we aren't," Stacey confirmed. "Going to go to The Pit again. Brent scored some whiskey from his dad's cabinet."

Cal looked at Brent who had since lowered his backpack off one shoulder and proceeded to pull the zipper back a few inches. Cal leaned over and peered inside. Sure enough, he caught the reflection of a bottle within.

He chewed the inside of his lip and was about to protest when Hank shoved the smokes up against his stomach.

With his shirt loose as it was, Hank misjudged the distance between them and the pack crumpled as it struck his belly.

Cal blushed again and took the pack from his friend's hand.

"What the fuck," he said, "Why not?"

Cal liked school, but he liked Stacey Mclernon more.

The Pit it is…

Chapter 2

"MY PARENTS ARE SQUARE as shit, you know that."

"Wait, your shit is square?" Hank said with a chuckle. He brought the bottle to his lips. "You should get that checked out."

Cal frowned and took a drag of his cigarette. It was almost noon, and he was starting to get hungry, which was making him irritable.

"No, what I mean is, they are just so damn boring. I mean, they're great and all. But *boring.*"

Cal's eyes moved to The Pit as he spoke, his gaze moving along the rim of the bowl. It had once been an active gravel pit, he knew, but it had long since been abandoned. When they had been younger, nine and ten instead of fifteen, the three of them used to race from the bottom to the top, sprinting all forty meters, at no less than a seventy-degree angle, until they collapsed on the dirt path, their chests heaving, sweat pouring down their cheeks.

Now, they just liked to look at the spot they affectionately called The Pit and think.

And talk.

And drink, smoke, whatever.

"All parents are boring," Stacey offered, grabbing the bottle from Hank. "It's kinda like their job to be boring."

Cal shrugged. Boring was fine, normal, even. But B*oring*? With a capital B. That was the worst.

"I guess."

For the next several minutes, they passed the bottle around in silence. Cal was beginning to feel buzzed, although he wasn't sure if this was from the alcohol or the cigarettes.

Or just on account of him being hungry.

"You guys ever think about what we'll be doing ten years from now? Twenty? I mean, this," Hank swished the bottle, and indicated the gravel pit with his chin. "is great, but will we still be coming back here when we're boring, too? When we have our own kids?"

The forward-thinking comment was so unlike Hank, that Cal had to do a double take to make sure that it wasn't Brent who had posed the question. As he watched, Hank scrunched his nose, moving his glasses back up to where they were supposed to be.

No, it had been Hank, and the boy appeared to be actually thinking about *it*.

About getting older.

For Cal, the answer was easy: if he was still in Mooreshead, South Carolina, when he was an adult, then he failed.

He wanted out, plain and simple.

Because Mooreshead, like his parents, was just too boring for him.

But Cal kept this little tidbit to himself. Instead, he offered, "Yeah, I think so. I mean, this place is cool, so why the fuck not?"

"We've had some good times here," Brent said softly. "You guys remember when we brought Trevor up here? Like six months ago?"

Cal chuckled.

Of course, he remembered. How could he forget how his stomach had hurt, first from the laughter and then from Trevor's fist.

"Yeah, he did a complete back roll down the side of The Pit," Hank replied with a chuckle of his own. "Fell all the way to the bottom. And you, Cal, I can't believe it was you that tricked him into walking backward toward the edge."

"Why? I can be—"

"Cuz you're a pussy," Hank said, laughing again. "And when Trevor punched you, I thought you were going to cry."

Cal stopped laughing.

"Fuck off, I wasn't going to cry. I was just laughing too hard, otherwise, I would have hit him back."

Hank rolled his eyes, but Cal didn't notice. His attention was focused on Stacey, who was staring down the side of the gravel pit, clearly disinterested in the boys' pissing contest.

"You? Take on Trever? I don't think so."

Cal felt his face go red, and looked away, distracting himself with a drag from his cigarette.

He inhaled too quickly and coughed.

"Whatever," he said after the irritation in his throat passed.

"I hope we come back here one day," Stacey said at last. "One day when we're old, but not boring. When the world has changed."

Cal's brow furrowed as he stared at her profile, marveling at how smooth her skin was.

Although he didn't have the same problem with acne that Hank did, Cal's skin always seemed a little bumpy to his touch. Stacey's, on the other hand, was as smooth as a sea-worn stone.

When the world has changed.

That, of course, was what Mrs. Johnson called a supposition. And with an image of his mother holding out his lunch, his father telling him to tuck in his shirt, burned into his mind, Cal figured it a bold one.

He wasn't sure that the world would ever change. And even if it did, there was no reason to believe that it would become anything but *boring*.

Boring, with a capital B. The worst kind.

Chapter 3

"HEY, YOU GUYS KNOW why they shut The Pit down?" Hank asked suddenly.

Both Cal and Brent shook their heads.

"Not this again," Stacey muttered.

They were lying on their backs staring upward, feeling the effects of the whiskey that they had nearly finished. Cal's eyelids were heavy, and he was slightly hypnotized by the way the clouds endlessly drifted across his vision. He felt like a child again, imagining fictional creatures hidden in their fluffy shapes.

"Come on, Stace. You know it's true," Hank continued. "My step-brother Matt told me that his friend used to work here, at The Pit, before the accident."

Cal's ears perked, and he pulled his eyes away from the clouds to look at his friend.

"Accident? What accident?"

Stacey groaned.

"Don't fall for it, Cal. It's just a stupid—"

"No, it's not stupid, it's true. My step-brother—"

Stacey rolled over and pushed herself onto her elbows, and Cal couldn't help peek into her shirt. His heart skipped a beat when he caught a glimpse of the tops of her small, firm breasts.

"The same step-brother who is high like ninety-percent of the time? That step-brother?"

Hank smiled.

"Yeah, that's the one. But he swears it's a true story."

Stacey flipped over and lay back down in the grass.

"Real reliable source, Hank."

Cal, his interest piqued, sat up.

"What story? What accident?"

He was amazed that during all fifteen years that he had lived in Mooreshead, and given the fact that he had been coming to The Pit for the better part of a decade, he had never heard anything about an 'accident'.

It was Hank who had first found the place. He was nine at the time, and it had never been made clear what he had been doing to stumble across it, but stumble he had. Fallen right in, actually. But instead of being upset, he had rushed to find Cal and tell him about the secret place he had discovered.

Back then, they had had to cut through Mr. Willingham's farm and the small forest bordering his lot in order to get to The Pit. It was easier now, what with Mr. Willingham getting so bored that he had spiced things up by putting the barrel end of a shotgun in his mouth a couple of years back, and they no longer felt like vagrant trespassers.

Several times Cal had asked his father about the place, but other than an *'oh, geez, I dunno Callum. It might be dangerous, you should probably steer clear of that place,'* or some facsimile, David Godfrey hadn't offered anything of substance.

Over time, Cal figured that his dad forgot about it, which was all the same to him. After all, this was their place to get away, to be free.

Still, he was perturbed that his father had never mentioned anything about an 'accident'.

Hank licked his lips and smirked. Stacey's dissension hadn't discouraged him from telling the story. If anything, it had encouraged him. The one thing Hank liked more than stealing and smoking his mother's du Maurier cigarettes was telling tales.

"Well," he began, "before I tell you about the accident, I think it's best if I start from the beginning."

Cal rolled his eyes. Hank didn't just love telling tales, he had a penchant for telling *long* tales. Long, rambling stories.

And he just knew that this was destined to be one of them.

"It all started years ago—maybe twenty, twenty-five years ago, the records aren't that clear—"

Stacey scoffed at the word 'records', but Hank ignored her.

"Anyway, back then the Mayor, Steven Partridge, managed to convince some developers to mine gravel from right here in Mooreshead. You see, the state was in the process of extending the highway system in South Carolina—specifically Interstate 26, I think—and they needed a massive amount of gravel to do it. Mooreshead wasn't the first choice, or even the fifth. Too wet, or some shit. But the thing is, Steven Partridge was determined. Back then Mooreshead wasn't as prosperous as it is now."

Even Hank had to chuckle at this. If the US was represented by a tennis ball, Mooreshead wouldn't even make up a single green hair. It had one high school, one fire station, four banks, and a God-fearing population of just under twelve thousand. Nothing about Mooreshead screamed *prosperity*.

"Yeah, I know, I can see it in your face. But you've gotta remember, this was a while back, twenty-five or so years ago. Times were different, then. Harder. No money, no jobs. Which is why Steven Partridge fought so hard to get the contract here, despite the fact that it was ludicrous to think that there would be enough gravel, what with Mooreshead being so close to the swamps. There's another, much longer story about what Steven had to do to get this contract, but that's another story for another day."

Hank visibly shuddered, and Cal made a mental note to ask his friend about this tale another time.

"Anyways, Mooreshead got the contract, and then things started to change, almost immediately."

"How?" Cal asked. For some reason, his heart was pounding away in his chest, and whatever fugue that the alcohol had brought on had since faded. He reached over and took another swig of the cheap scotch, grimacing at the burning sensation that cascaded all the way down to his stomach.

"Well, for one, Steven was heralded as a hero. Knighted, almost. Got everything he could have wanted, because the townsfolk finally had jobs. Work meant money, and money meant food and entertainment. Survival. Anyways, the town flourished. Really, it wasn't like it is now; for the seventies, it was fucking booming. Las fucking Vegas, baby. But not everyone was happy about the change. The church, for one, wasn't a fan of the strip clubs, bars, and gambling halls that opened up as soon as The Pit started to become operational. Shit, you guys know the church…" Hank let his sentence trail off. There were some things that couldn't be said, not even here, in their sanctuary. "Let's just say that these two *ideas* of Mooreshead started to clash. Steven himself became the primary target for the church, given that he was often seen at the brothels, or drunk off his ass. But here's the thing: he could pretty much do whatever he wanted. As long as the mine stayed open, and there was work to be had, he was going to be re-elected, no matter what the church said about it."

Hank reached over and grabbed the bottle from Cal and gulped greedily. Then he took his time lighting up a cigarette, before laying his head back on the grass and continuing.

"There was a priest back then, a man by the name of Father McCabe. You know Father Link from the school chapel?"

Cal nodded, recalling the kind, young man who always wore the same pair of faded jeans with his white collar and black shirt. The man was gentle, funny, more laid back than any pastor he had ever come in contact with.

"Well, Father McCabe was pretty much the exact opposite of Father Link. And Father McCabe was out to get the mayor, some would say no matter the cost. But even Father McCabe wasn't powerful enough to stop the mayor, not yet anyway. Not until... not until the men started to dig deeper, and deeper, until they found something in The Pit, something old, something man-made. That, my dear friends, was when the real trouble started."

Chapter 4

"GOTTA PISS," HANK SAID suddenly, rising to his feet.

"Wait—what? What happened? What did they find?"

"Hold your horses, Cal. Lemme piss first."

Cal stared as Hank started to walk toward a cluster of trees a dozen yards from where he sat.

"Fuck—c'mon!"

"He always tells it this way," Stacey said quietly, drawing his attention. She was still lying on her back, her eyes closed. He liked her like this; this way he could observe her without risking being caught.

"What way? What do you mean."

"Leaves halfway through the story. Makes you wait. And then tells the stupid part."

"Stupid part?"

Stacey opened her eyes, turned her head, and squinted at him in the hot sun. Cal had been staring at the front of her shirt as he spoke, and he quickly raised his eyes to look her in the face. He tried to fight the color that rose in his cheeks, but lost. But Stacey didn't appear to notice, or if she did, she didn't care.

Or maybe she liked it, Cal thought. It wasn't that far-fetched an idea, was it? After all, Stacey was pretty. Not beautiful, no, but close.

Cal and Hank and Brent on the other hand? They were average at best. Maybe she hung out with them because of the attention she got.

"Yeah, it gets real dumb now," Stacey said with an air of boredom. "I looked it up, you know. Went to the library. Couldn't find out anything except that there *was* a Mayor Steven Partridge. But this Father McCabe? No record."

She turned her head back to the sky again and shut her eyes.

"Which is why I call bullshit. Anyways, you'll see."

Cal chewed the inside of his lip, then addressed Brent who lay to his left.

"What do you think, Brent?" when the boy didn't answer, Cal turned to him and was surprised to see that was sleeping. "Brent? Brent, wake the fuck up."

Brent's eyes snapped open, and a confused look crossed his face.

"Wha—what? What happened?" he asked groggily.

Hank chuckled.

"Nothing happened," he said as he returned from voiding his bladder. "Except maybe you having a wet dream."

"Fuck off, I was just dozing. It's your boring ass story that did it to me, anyway."

Hank laughed, and then sat on the grass.

"Well, what happened? What did the machines hit?" Cal demanded.

Hank lit another smoke and took several long, slow drags before finally bringing his eyes up to meet Cal's.

"You really want to know, Cal? I mean, once you hear this, you can't *un*hear it."

Cal rolled his eyes, and Brent groaned.

"Just fucking tell me."

Hank had a twinkle in his eye when he spoke next.

"Well, let me first set the scene…"

***

"Two years passed since they started digging, and the town was flourishing. But it couldn't last, everyone knew that there was only limited gravel in Mooreshead. Mayor Partridge knew this, and he also knew that the second the money dried up, that the jobs that he had brought were no longer available, he was as good as dead. And, of course, the rest of the sins that came with the money—the strip clubs, the gambling halls, the bars—well they would go, too. When rumors hit town that they had dug as deep as they could, Steven Partridge pleaded with the company to keep on digging. When the company refused, saying that it was dangerous to go any deeper, he decided to go out to the site himself.

"Now, keep in mind that at this point, Steven Partridge had ballooned up to nearly three-hundred pounds, and he had developed a taste in fine clothing— bespoke three-piece suits in particular. So, imagine this guy, showing up here, at The Pit, to tell the men of Mooreshead how to do their jobs. These were hard men, men with faces smeared with dirt, burdened with perpetual coughs and nicotine stains that ran all the way to their bones. Yeah, Steven's approach didn't go over well. Still, he offered the men bonuses, raises, if they kept on digging. He promised to shower them with money that he, nor the town, actually had—that didn't exist. But Steven was obsessed with the lifestyle that he had obtained and refused to let it go. Money makes the world go 'round, Cal. Money. Nothing but money."

Hank paused and took a drag of his cigarette.

"And? What'd they do?"

"They kept on digging, of course. They kept on digging until they hit something."

"Struck a pile of shit, just like this story," Stacey snorted. Brent, who had managed to keep his eyes open for this chapter, laughed.

"Very funny," Hank scowled. "The truth is, no one really knows exactly what they hit. I mean, they didn't have cameras back then, not like the ones we have now. Anyways, if there were any photos taken, then the FBI would have confiscated them."

Cal's eyes went wide.

"The FBI?"

Hank nodded.

"Yeah, but I'm getting ahead of myself. Anyways, there were seven people working in The Pit when they struck the *thing*, and reports of what they actually hit are mixed. Some say that they hit a hunk of ore in the earth, a giant piece of metal. Others say that it was just rock, while some still say that they didn't hit anything, that the men were just sick of digging. But the story that made its way back to Father McCabe in town was that they had hit a tunnel of sorts. A portal, maybe, a passage."

Cal squinted hard, trying to determine if his friend was just pulling his leg.

"A passage?"

"See?" Stacey mocked. "Told you so, Cal. Told you, you were wasting your time."

Cal ignored her, his eyes now locked on Hank's.

"A passage? A passage to where?"

Hank took a final drag of his cigarette before flicking it into the gravel pit. Cal's eyes followed it with strange fascination, watching the glowing ember float through the air until it descended out of view.

When he turned back, he was surprised to see that Hank was staring at him.

"A passage to Hell, Cal. They say that the men had unearthed a passage to Hell."

Chapter 5

"HELL? LIKE *THE* HELL?"

Hank laughed, but Brent wasn't amused. He stood, wobbled on his feet, and then screwed up his face.

"I'm not listening to this shit," he said quietly. "This blasphemous nonsense."

Hank held up his narrow palms defensively, his dark eyebrows rising up his forehead.

"I'm just telling the story! Don't shoot the messenger!"

"Well Stacey is right, it's garbage. A fairy tale full of lies— did they find seven gnomes down there, Hank? A sleeping princess?"

Brent started to walk away as he spoke, his back toward the dirt path that led to the mouth of the gravel pit, when Stacey hopped to her feet.

"I'm going with Brent. I've heard this so many times, anyway," she said with a flick of her long blond hair.

Cal was conflicted; part of him wanted to go with Brent and Stacey, particularly the latter, but the story was enthralling no matter how far-fetched it had gotten. He glanced from Stacey to Hank, who still held his hands up as if instructed by an officer of the law. There was a sparkle in his eyes, one that seemed to draw Cal in.

Instead of following after Stacey, who continued to stare down at him expectantly, he reached for the pack of cigarettes that rested on the ground beside Hank. He slipped one out and put it to his lips.

"I'll catch up with you in a few—after this smoke."

Stacey shrugged and offered a wan smile.

Was that disappointment in her face? Did she really want me to come?

Cal stared at her ass in her school skirt as she hurried away from him, trying to catch up with Brent. His mouth full of smoke, he turned back to Hank.

"You like her, don't you?" Hank said, smiling widely, revealing teeth that were just a little too large for his mouth.

Cal felt his ears getting hot again, and it was all he could do to stop his entire face from turning into a tomato.

"Shut up," he said.

Hank finally lowered his hands.

"Meh, it's okay. We all know it."

Cal swallowed hard.

"All?"

"Ha, yeah. Me, Brent—Stacey. Whatever, she likes you, too."

"Really?" the word came out almost as a gasp. "She said that?"

Hank shook his head.

"No, but I can tell."

Cal took another drag from the cigarette. In his excitement, he pulled in too much smoke and then started to cough. Hank reached over and smacked him on the back hard enough that Cal winced.

"Fuck off, just get on with the story," he said after regaining his breath.

He's messing with me... Stacey doesn't like me, at least not like that. Not pudgy Callum Godfrey.

Hank, still smiling, took a swig from the bottle of whiskey and continued.

"Right, so, where was I?"

"Passage to Hell," Cal said quickly. "They dug too deep, and breached a passage to Hell."

Cal's eyes drifted out over the empty gravel pit as he spoke. It was large, about fifty meters across, and extended at least forty or so meters into the earth. Covered with a thin layer of sand—sand he knew to be soft from back in the days when they used to run up and down the embankment—it was an impressive sight. His eyes continued down the side, which was now starting to become overrun by tree roots, and to the center. He knew little of gravel pits, but for some reason, he had always expected it to end in a point, like the end of a freshly sharpened pencil. Only it didn't. Instead, the bottom was blunted, like the inside of a thimble.

Did they really hit something here? In Mooreshead?

He tried to transport himself into the seventies, into Mayor Partridge in his fancy suit shouting at tired looking men with heavily-lined faces to keep on digging, the lights from mini-Vegas in the distance reflecting off his wide eyes.

Keep on diggin'! Don't y'all stop diggin' now! Money, 'tis what makes the world go round and what makes yer shovels and your contraptions there keep on diggin'!

"Ah, yes, how could I forget."

And then his friend continued his story, and true to Stacey's word, it slowly digressed into something that could only be regarded as pure fiction.

Chapter 6

"IT WAS MIDDAY WHEN the digger struck the object in the earth... whatever it was. And when it did, it started a collapse. The sand and digger and the two men operating it started to get sucked into the pit. Kinda like quicksand, you know? Anyway, the other five men came rushing, trying to help the workers who had somehow managed to climb out of the digger. But the sand was rushing too hard, too fast, sinking into the hole in the earth. The men on the sides of the pit threw ropes, threw anything and everything they could find. But the hole just kept getting bigger and bigger, until it eventually swallowed the two men and the digger whole."

"What happened to them? The men?" Cal gasped.

Hank shook his head, the smile that had been on his face from the outset of the tale sliding off his acne-ridden face.

"The men who were sucked into the hole were as good as dead—the sand and gravel just kept piling on top of them, suffocating and crushing them. One of the other men jumped in and tried to save them, but he too was buried. The others ran to call the police. Only the police never came."

"Who came?"

"At first, nobody. And then the men started to freak out. You see, the hole was still sucking in dirt, and many of the men were very religious, at least when it came to things like this. Anyways, they thought that maybe the entire earth was going to fall into that hole." Hank shrugged. "I'm not really sure what they thought the cops might do if that were the case, but I'm guessing they just wanted the comfort of authority. Instead, they got the Mayor."

"Mayor Partridge?"

Hank nodded.

"Yep—either he intercepted the police call, or maybe he had just paid off dispatch to let him know if and when any calls from the gravel pit came in. I mean, it was dangerous work back then, and with the pressure that the Mayor was putting on everyone to keep on digging, it was only a matter of time before an accident happened. And from a PR standpoint, the Mayor would have wanted to keep on top of these things. Especially with Father McCabe breathing down his neck.

"Anyways, when Mayor Partridge showed up, that's when things got really weird."

Cal scoffed.

"How can it—"

But Hank held up a hand, cutting him off.

"Trust me, it can and does gets stranger. For one, the men who fell into the hole?"

Cal nodded, picturing their mouths wide with screams before being chocked by thousands of pounds of sand and dirt and gravel.

"Well, the mayor came to the pit at least ten minutes after they had been buried."

"Yeah? And?"

"And when he arrived, they just started to climb back out again."

Hank let the word hang in the air like a foul smell. Eventually, Cal broke the silence.

"Wait... they climbed out again? I thought the sand was falling in..."

"No, you don't get it. The men who climbed out again were dead already. They were fucking dead, Cal."

Cal's heart skipped a beat as he tried to comprehend what his friend was saying, now understanding why Stacey had said what she had. What had started as a history lesson of the town in which they lived, and the gravel pit that they frequented, had since degenerated into a zombie tale.

And yet there was something compelling about his friend's words. Something that held Cal's tongue when his first instinct was to tell Hank to fuck off, to stop talking bullshit.

"What—what do you mean they were dead?" he asked instead.

"They were dead. D-E-A-D. Shit, you can't spend ten minutes or more buried over your head in sand and survive, Cal."

"What if there was an air pocket, or something? I mean, the sand was spilling in."

"They were dead, Cal. The story goes that they were fucked up looking when they came out, their eyes completely black. They crawled out of the pit, grabbed the other men and pulled them down with them. Except for Mayor Partridge—somehow the fat bastard managed to stay out of their way. Shit, he probably threw the men down into the pit as a sort of sacrifice to save his own hide."

Cal blinked hard.

"They... they pulled them down?"

Hank nodded.

"Yep. Pulled them down with the rest of the sand that continued to pour in. Mayor Partridge would have gotten away completely, but then Father McCabe showed up. No one knows how he found out about the accident out at The Pit—maybe he just sensed it, you know? He was a priest after all. Maybe he got wind on the papal phone that a gateway had opened. Anyways, when he arrived, Mayor Partridge intercepted him. The priest could still see the men being dragged under the sand, the sunlight reflecting off their black eyes. He tried to perform an exorcism of sorts, right then and there. But Mayor Partridge was having none of it. He was still obsessed with the town, the money, the gambling, the whores. You know, all the fun things that came with The Pit. Some say that he would have just claimed it never happened, that the workers just abandoned the sight. But Father McCabe... he was a problem, one that wasn't easy to solve."

Hank paused to take another drink. Then he looked over his shoulder to The Pit.

"Have you ever been here when it rains?" he asked absently.

The question took Cal by surprise, and he had to think about it for a moment before answering.

"Yeah, I guess. I mean, we used to come here all the time as kids. I'm sure it rained sometimes."

Hank shook his head.

"No, I mean when it's really pouring. Like tsunami-style rain."

Cal couldn't remember, and he said as much.

Hank brought the bottle to his lips again and swallowed long and hard.

"I have," he said, all the humor gone from his voice. "I've been here when it's really pouring. And I tell you, the water does some weird shit down there at the bottom of The Pit. It starts to froth and foam, kinda like a tiny sea, you know? A mini ocean."

Cal had no fucking clue what Hank was talking about.

He shook his head.

"Wait—what happened to the Mayor and the priest?"

Hank shuddered and with a groan, he stood.

"Mayor Partridge threw him into The Pit with the others. No amount of prayers could save him—like the seven workers that day, Father McCabe suffocated on the sand. Or at least, that's how the story goes. None of the bodies were ever found."

"None of them?"

Hank grimaced.

"None of them," he confirmed.

"What about Mayor Partridge? The sand pit? Did it stop fall-ing in?"

"No one has heard from Mayor Partridge since," Hank cast his arm over The Pit, turning his back to Cal. "As for The Pit? Some say that Hell was satisfied that day, that enough bodies fell into Satan's mouth to fill his belly for a time."

Hank took another pull from the bottle, finishing the last drop. Then he reared back and threw it as far as he could into the gravel pit.

"Hank! What—"

"But you know what I think, Cal? I think that it's only a mat-ter of time before the gates to Hell open once again. And I want to be as far away as possible when that happens."

Chapter 7

THE WHISKEY WAS GONE, and Hank and Cal shared the final cigarette in silence.

Cal didn't—*couldn't*—believe the story, but as he stared out over The Pit, his mind started to superimpose images of the workers being sucked down into the hole, of Mayor Partridge in his three-piece tossing Father McCabe to his death.

He *couldn't* believe the story, but that didn't stop him from thinking about a priest and a Mayor at odds with the way that Mooreshead was being commandeered by greed and sin. Of digging too deep. Of eight men dead, and one missing.

Of a frothy, gateway to Hell.

His heart was racing.

This wasn't the Mooreshead that he knew. This wasn't *any-thing* like the Mooreshead that he knew.

Hank's story wasn't true, of course, but that didn't matter so much to Cal. Or maybe it wasn't *all* true. But Cal knew that with stories, even urban legends such as this one, beneath the layers of lies and exaggerations, there was always some truth buried beneath. Sometimes you had to dig as deep as they had in The Pit, but with enough hard work, you could unearth the truth.

And even if it had all just been a feud between the Mayor and a man of the cloth, well, that was more excitement than he could have even fathomed for Mooreshead, which was boring with a capital B.

Cal was going to dig alright, and like the men in the pit, he was going to keep on going, with or without the staunch en-couragement of a fancy dressing mayor.

A smile crossed his round face.

***

"How was school today, Cal?" his mother asked from across the table.

"Fine," Cal replied quickly, shoveling another forkful of pasta into his mouth. Every time he lied, he knew that he started to ramble and couldn't help himself.

Filling his mouth seemed to be the best way to keep quiet.

He was fifteen, going on sixteen, and next year he would move out. He had saved up some money working at the local hardware store and based on his waning attention and less than stellar attendance record, college was out of the question. Even if he had been a straight-A student, however, he wasn't interested; the last thing that he wanted to do was go to a three-hundred-year-old institution that taught the same shit year in and year out.

The idea rivaled even Mooreshead boredom.

Except...

Cal swallowed his bolus of pasta.

"Hey Dad, you ever hear about a feud between the Mayor and a Priest?"

David Godfrey didn't even look up from his plate. A soft-spoken man with a copper-colored mustache and thinning hair, David was a man of few words. He was a good father, Cal supposed, but by God was he boring.

"Mayor? Of Mooreshead?"

"Yeah, a while back. Like in the seventies, maybe."

David took a sip of his beer.

"Only Mayor I know is Mayor Turnbull. Been the Mayor for as long as I can remember."

Cal made a face, but his father's answer didn't come as a surprise. Like everything about his family, about Mooreshead, it was predictable.

He turned to his mother next.

"Mom? What about you?"

She hesitated before answering. It lasted only long enough to twitch, but it wasn't like his mother not to answer immediately. Regardless of the query, she always shot back an answer; she was confident, if occasionally ill-informed.

"No."

Cal stared at her for a moment, and for once she was the one to look away first.

She's lying.

Still, his mother was a tough nut to crack. Lying or not, he could tell by the way her lips were pressed together that he wasn't going to get any more out of her.

Cal turned back to his father, who was slowly twirling his fork into his spaghetti.

"What about the gravel pit, Dad? You ever hear anything about the gravel pit?"

David Godfrey's eyes shot up.

"What gravel pit?"

"You know the old Forrester Gravel Pit behind Mr. Willingham's farm? Just south of Kinkairn?"

David stopped twirling his fork, and his eyes darkened.

"I told you not to go up there."

Cal recoiled.

"No, you didn't. You said I should probably steer clear —"

"Yes, I did. Cal, that place is… is…"

Cal leaned forward now, squinting.

"Is what?"

David lowered his gaze and started twirling his fork again.

"Nothing. You just shouldn't be up there."

"Why not?"

It was his mother who answered.

"Cal, just leave it alone. It's dangerous up there."

"Dangerous? I used to go up there all the time as a kid. It's a fucking abandoned gravel pit. What's so dangerous about it?"

"Watch your language, son."

Cal dropped his fork, and it clanged loudly on his porcelain plate.

"Aw shucks, dad. I'm not seven anymore. I'm fifteen. And next year, I'll be out of this place."

The words came out of his mouth in such a flurry that he was unable to stop them. His throat was hoarse from all the cigarettes, and he wasn't convinced that the whiskey he had drunk pretty much all day was out of his system yet.

"Cal? What do you mean, you're out of this place? We've talked about this."

He looked at his mother's sad eyes, but instead of feeling guilty, for some reason, her expression infuriated him even further.

"What? Can't I even ask a question around here? Have an opinion about something?" he stood quickly, nearly toppling his chair behind him. "Fuck it, I'm going to bed. See you in the morning."

And then he left the kitchen, his ears getting hot. But Cal didn't even make it upstairs before the nagging feeling of guilt about the way that he acted started to eat at him.

It wasn't his parents' fault. They were good people. Boring, predictable, but essentially good. Good to him, good to each other.

But then Cal thought of Hank's story and his parent's strange reaction to his questions, and the guilt suddenly started to fade.

Chapter 8

CAL DIDN'T GO TO school the next day either. But instead of meeting up with Hank and Brent, he purposefully avoided their usual meeting spot. A little birdie had told him that Stacey was attending class that day, as her parents had found out that they had skipped the day before. It was only by some miracle that Stacey's parents hadn't reached out to his own.

Although he wanted to see Stacey again—he always wanted to see Stacey—he was grateful that she wasn't around. She would be a distraction, and today he was on a mission.

Cal headed deeper into town, away from The Pit, bowing his head to avoid being noticed by any of his mother's friends who spent their days shopping. He wasn't interested in any of the shops or restaurants, despite the fact that his stomach was already grumbling; instead, Cal went to the only place that he hated more than school.

He went to the library.

Mooreshead's single library stood pretty much in the direct center of town. Cal remembered hearing somewhere—history class, maybe—that it had been erected on the day that the town was founded, nearly sixty years earlier, as a sort of cornerstone of the community.

That and the church, of course.

Looking up at the brick structure, complete with cracks that ran deep into the foundation and a massive clock tower that hadn't moved or chimed since... well, since *ever*, Cal couldn't help but scowl.

Boring, boring, boring, boring...

Glancing around, equally concerned now that he would be spotted by one of his mother's friends as one of his own, Cal slunk even lower into the collar of his shirt until he resembled a bipedal tortoise. Then he slinked up the marble steps to the front door, gave a final, cursory look, and then pulled it wide and slipped inside.

Twice he had been in the library: the first time he was just a young boy, seven, maybe eight years old, and his mother had dragged him to the place in search of a recipe of all things. The second time had been a few years back as part of a class outing.

A visit to the local library qualified as a field trip in Mooreshead, permission slips and all.

Now, on this third occasion, Cal wasn't at all surprised that it was exactly the way he remembered it: reeking of wet wood, dust motes as large as bumblebees clouding his vision.

And dark. Jesus, the damn place was so dark that Cal would have had a hard time finding his pecker if he had to piss. Hank said that the reason why it was so dark had to do with the type of wiring in the ancient building—knob and tube, or something—that couldn't handle the light bulbs of today.

If The Pit was still open, there would be plenty of money to upgrade the wiring, he thought incomprehensibly.

Clearing the dust from in front of his face by waving a hand, he looked around while he waited for his eyes to adjust to the dim lighting.

Predictably, the library's only patrons were the long-dead authors of the books that lined the walls and ascended to the ceiling, nearly twenty feet above. The thick desks were all unoccupied, their wooden surfaces so reflective that they appeared to have been lacquered that very morning.

Nary a fingerprint in sight, let alone another human.

Cal cleared his throat as his eyes wandered up the walls of books. Unlike other libraries that he had seen on TV, the practical ones, there were no metal racks arranged in rows that housed alphabetically organized books, making it easy to find what you were looking for. Instead, in Mooreshead Library, the books lined the perimeter walls, each of which made up about thirty feet of the perfect square. There was a ladder on a track that he remembered from previous visits squeaked like a maimed mouse as it slid all the way around the room. Toward the back, there was a single desk with a green lamp on it. The surface was completely void of anything—a pen, paper, *book*—save a shining silver bell.

Cal refused to ring the bell. There was one outside the Principal's office, and if the secretary wasn't there, you had to ring it to let Mr. Malhorn know you'd arrived. He would then wait for a minute or two to give the pretense of being busy before coming out of his office, a stupid, smug smile on his face.

The only reason Cal went to the office was when he was ordered there by one of his teachers, so for him, the sound of the bell had a sort of Pavlovian implication.

No, he definitely didn't want to ring the bell.

And yet the idea of searching through the floor to ceiling rows of books for some obscure facts—or fictions, Hank's story was about ninety-percent bullshit—about Mooreshead history was even more appalling to him. Making up his mind, Cal strode over to the desk and peered over the other side, hoping that the librarian was, for no reason whatsoever, sitting on the floor.

She, or he, wasn't.

Cal glanced back and forth.

"Hello?" he said at last. Even though he had barely muttered the word, it sounded impossibly loud to him, reverberating off the stained-glass windows with a force reminiscent of a strong gale. "Jesus," he whispered, but this word seemed to travel even faster and louder than the previous.

Cal made a disgusted face and shook his head.

Maybe I should just leave, get the fuck out of here. Go to school for once.

But the story...

Cringing even as his arm reached out, Cal brushed the top of the bell as gingerly as possible. If his words had been gale force, the ringing bell was like a shotgun blast at a funeral.

The sound was so loud that Cal literally jumped backward and covered his ears with his hands.

Tinnitus ongoing, which he was now fairly certain a product of his first ever hangover, Cal half-expected a trapdoor behind the desk to fly open and a white-bearded librarian to emerge from a cloud of thick smoke.

But this was Mooreshead, and nothing interesting happens in Mooreshead.

Except...

"Calm down, fella. I was just taking a piss."

The words were uttered in the same tone that Cal himself had used, but with the damn echo, they sounded like the musings of a giant. Heart racing, Cal whipped around, but when he saw the man who had spoken, his anxiety abated.

"What can I do for you?"

Cal opened his mouth to say something, but then closed it again. He had met the librarian previously, both times that he had been in the library, in fact, and this was not *her*.

Those times, it had been a short woman with curly brown hair who reeked of mothballs and alcohol. But the man who stood before him now was young, just a handful of years older than Cal himself, with shaggy blond hair and a goatee.

The man stared back at Cal, waiting for him to speak. Eventually, Cal got over the shock.

"Sorry, I was... I was looking for the librarian."

The man crossed his arms over his thin chest and pushed his lips together defiantly.

"You're looking at him. What can I do for you?"

Cal's eyebrows knitted.

"What happened to—happened to—what—" but for the life of him he couldn't think of the previous librarian's name.

The man just watched him sputter, a strange expression on his face. Cal sighed, and then took a deep breath, deciding that it didn't matter what happened to the other librarian, or if this kid worked here.

It was best to just get to the point.

"I'm here to—" he started, but the man broke into a smile, revealing a set of large, white teeth.

"Lemme guess, you want to know about Father McCabe and Mayor Partridge?"

Cal's brow furrowed.

"Wh—wha—" he stammered, "How did you know?"

Chapter 9

"IT'S NOT MAGIC," THE man laughed. "A guy like you? Looking around like a fucking bank robber before entering the library? There's only one reason why someone like you would come in here."

Cal breathed deeply, and then immediately regretted the decision as the pungent scent of mold coated his nose and throat.

The man pushed a lock of blond hair behind his ear and leaned forward expectantly.

"Am I right?" he whispered with a grin.

Cal nodded.

"You're right. I just—I heard this story about Mooreshead and the gravel pit, you know? The, uhh, the Forrester Gravel Pit."

The librarian smirked.

"Yeah, I've heard a lot of bullshit stories about that place, too."

Cal's heart sank.

"So, it's not true?"

The man shrugged.

"I didn't say that."

When Cal screwed up his face, the man softened and held out his hand.

"What's your name, kid?"

"Cal."

Cal shook the man's outstretched hand. To his surprise, his grip was much stronger than his thin frame suggested.

"Seth Parsons," the man said, raising his arms and waving them about the room. "Curator of the Mooreshead Town Library."

Cal raised an eyebrow.

"Curator? I thought you said—"

Seth shrugged.

"Meh, Curator, Librarian, what's the difference? The title has legal ramifications. Anyhoo, you wanna know about the town's history?"

He paused for a moment, and Cal felt uncomfortable as Seth eyed him suspiciously.

"Ah, of course not. You only want to know about the feud, am I right?"

Cal felt his face redden. There was something about the way Seth could read him like a book, look not only into him, but through him, that was strangely off-putting and embarrassing.

"Yeah, I'm right. Of course, I'm right. Here, come with me."

With that, Seth turned and started to walk toward the ladder near the far side of the room. Cal, still confused over what was happening, followed.

What the hell have I gotten myself into?

Cal half-expected Seth to start up the wooden ladder, grab a book at the very top of the shelves, perhaps a dusty volume that was twice the size of the other books, and bring it down to him, grinning a jester's grin.

But that was his imagination running amok.

Again.

Instead, Seth grabbed a book off one of the lower shelves. It was a green book, about the size of a hardcover novel, only with a soft jacket.

But it was far from an ordinary book. As far as Cal could tell, there was no writing on the cover, no title, no author, nothing.

"That's it? This is the story of Father McCabe and Mayor Partridge?"

Seth laughed, but didn't answer straight away. Instead, he led Cal to one of the empty desks and pulled a chair out for him.

Cal sat while Seth took the seat across from him and laid the book in the center of the table.

"This is the book?" Cal repeated.

Seth laughed again, but this time he answered.

Sort of.

"No, the story isn't in the book." He brought a finger and pointed at his temple. "It's in here."

Cal made a face.

"What?"

He tapped his temple.

"In here."

Cal leaned back in his chair, wondering if this whole day was just a consequence of his hangover.

Do hangovers do that? He wondered. *Do they make you see things? Turn normal things, like visiting the library, into some sort of mind fuck?*

If they did, then Cal was prepared to swear off alcohol from this day forward.

Why didn't I just go to The Pit with Hank and Brent?

Cal sighed, and then made up his mind.

"I'm sorry, but I have to go."

Seth laughed again, but when Cal went to stand, the man reached out and grabbed his arm. His grip wasn't aggressive, at least not overtly so, but his touch felt strange and Cal instinctively tried to pull away.

He couldn't.

Cal looked down at those fingers, which suddenly seemed watery, as if they weren't made of skin and bone, but some sort of liquid.

He gulped down the bile that splashed up his esophagus.

As he watched, Seth's fingers started to change color, to become almost like a heat map, all reds and yellows and oranges.

"Wha—"

The man hushed him, but while the sound itself was normal enough, there was something *beneath* that sound, something that followed on its heels. Even though Cal was staring at the man's face, and he could clearly see that his mouth, lips, and tongue were no longer moving, the *hush* sound, more of a *shhh* now, continued on... and on... and on...

It was as if he were hearing waves crash softly on a beach.

Just as Cal felt an overwhelming calmness wash over, an instant before he was certain he would smell the brine of the sea, Seth let go of his hand and he snapped back to reality.

All he smelled now was that rotting wood aroma.

Cal collapsed in his seat with a deep, shuddering breath.

"I think you should stay," Seth said tucking a lock of hair behind his ear. He smiled broadly. "Just for a little while longer... what do you think?"

Cal swallowed hard and winced as the bile receded back to the pit of his stomach.

"Just a little while longer," he whispered. "Just a little longer."

Chapter 10

SETH LISTENED CLOSELY AS Cal recounted the tale of the Mayor and the priest, as was told to him by Hank. He tried to get as many of the details as he could correct, even going as far as to use Hank's exact words in some cases, but he wasn't sure he did it justice.

Cal's head still didn't feel *right* ever since Seth had grabbed his arm, and he was grateful that he had once again taken up residence across from him.

The Curator stared at him intently as he spoke, a smirk on his face. Cal, on the other hand, had a hard time keeping his eyes locked on Seth's; they kept drifting to the green book in the center of the table.

The one with no title, no author.

It took all his willpower to resist reaching out and flipping it open, inhaling the words desperately like a suffocating man given a straw full of oxygen.

Cal finished the story with the mayor tossing the priest into The Pit, but skimmed over the part about a doorway opening and the workers coming back, their eyes black and chalky like coal briquettes; that was too much.

That was just Hank's bullshitting.

Cal cleared his throat and stared sheepishly across the table, leveling his eyes at Seth, trying to gauge the man's opinion of him, of the story.

Does he think I'm crazy? Am I crazy?

He started to second guess himself, cursing internally for telling the story as if it were fact.

I should have laughed… I should have laughed when I told about Mayor Partridge in his three-piece suit ordering the workers around like a regal Humpty Dumpty. I should have made it clear that I think this is all a stupid joke. Just a dumb joke made up by Hank who was jealous because I have a thing for Stacey, and Stacey has a thing for me.

But Seth wasn't laughing. In fact, Seth wasn't doing *anything*. He simply sat there, hands clasped on the table in front of him, the smirk still on his young, handsome face.

Cal waited about thirty seconds before leaning forward and breaking the silence.

"Well? Have you heard this story before? Is it..." Cal could barely force the word out, "...is it *true*?"

Seth slowly separated his hands and placed his palms flat on the table.

"It's true," he said, with a small nod.

Cal felt the air exit his lungs in an audible *whoosh.*

Seth chuckled.

"It's true," he repeated. His laugh slowly transformed from a snicker into a full-blown bellow. "It's true... it's true... it's... it's..."

Seth's laughter became so all-encompassing that he could no longer get the words out. Cal, his face as white as a sheet, watched the man in abject horror.

For a fleeting moment, he wondered if there was something in the air in Mooreshead Town Library, something other than dust and the foul reek of wet paper and rot. He had heard once that casinos not only pumped oxygen into the air to keep people awake, but that they sometimes pumped something else too, a little *je ne sais quoi*, to keep people happy as they blew their last dollar on a whim and a prayer.

Maybe something like that was happening here; maybe this strange man with the long blond hair had pumped some strong, odorless dope into the air and this was making everything so... *strange.*

"I'm sorry," he said without thinking.

Seth immediately stopped laughing and his expression became flat.

"You're sorry? Why are you sorry?"

Cal, taken aback by the sudden change in expression, blubbered something incoherent.

He was feeling dizzy again, dizzy and nauseous.

"Why?" Seth demanded again, his eyes boring into Cal.

"I—I dunno," he stammered, "Why—why are you laughing?"

Seth simply stared at him, and Cal, fearful now that he had offended the strange man, fought the instinct to apologize a second time.

"Seth?"

Seth brought a finger and pointed to his head again.

"It's funny, because you already knew that the story was true shortly after you stepped inside the library. I mean, you knew it when I did this," he pointed at his head. "When I said the story was in here."

Cal, confused, scrunched up his face.

"Oh, I see. You thought I meant that it was in *here*, as in inside *my* head. Ahh, that makes sense."

Seth leaned forward and Cal instinctively drew back.

"Cal, the stories are real once they form in your head. Not mine. *Yours*."

"Wh—what?"

The Leporidae *burrow is long and deep…*

The thought appeared in Cal's mind, materialized, as all thoughts do, out of nothing. But this was different. It didn't feel like *his* thought. For one, he had no clue what the hell a *Leporidae* was.

It was as if it had been placed there.

He shook his head, trying to rid himself of the strange word, and when he raised his gaze to look at Seth, the man was smiling again.

"Long and deep, Callum Godfrey. Long and deep."

"What—how did you know my last name?" Once again, Cal's heart was jackhammering away in his chest. "What the fuck is going on here?"

Seth's smile grew.

"You think that Mooreshead is boring, but you're wrong about that, Cal. *That* is simply a story that you have woven. The truth is, there are places on this earth—Mooreshead, Askergan, Stumphole Swamp, Scarsdale, Seaforth, Pinedale Hospital, Father Callahan's church—that mark doorways to other worlds, Cal."

The Leporidae *burrow is long and deep...*

"What are you talking about?" his words came out in a tight whisper.

Seth nodded solemnly and continued.

"These doorways were built long ago—a long, *long* time ago. Even before me, Cal. And these doors... they must remain closed. Father McCabe made a sacrifice to save Mooreshead, and others have done the same in Askergan County and in the Swamp, although they don't know it yet. Your time will come to write another story, a different story—and you too will make a sacrifice."

Cal felt a heavy wave of dizziness wash over him, culminating in a bout of nausea that brought bile into his throat.

"I'm going—I think I'm going to be sick," he said, pushing back from the table. He gagged and then burped, but nothing came forth.

Seth was suddenly by his side, leaning in close.

Don't touch me… please if you touch me I'm going to puke every-where…

Seth didn't touch him.

"Open the book, Cal. Read your story," his voice was soft, quiet.

Cal closed his eyes for a moment, and the sickness slowly passed.

Open the book.

Cal opened his eyes and focused on the dusty green cover in front of him. A few moments ago, he had been chomping at the bit to open it, but now he felt a strong aversion. After all the strange things that had happened since arriving in the library, somehow he just knew that none of this would compare to what would happen if he opened that book.

He thought briefly of his mother, her smooth, caring face, her kind eyes, holding his brown paper lunch bag, telling him to tuck in his shirt.

Cal knew that if he opened the book, he would no longer be boring with a capital B—his life would change. Maybe not right away, maybe not for a while, but something deep down told him that he would never be the same again.

He swallowed hard, forcing images of his family seated at the dinner table out of his mind. With a shaking hand, he reached out and gripped the green cover between thumb and forefinger.

Then Cal opened it.

Chapter 11

CAL MOANED SOFTLY AND then rubbed his wrist. His hand was cramped, his fingers ached.

There was something in the library air, there had to be.

"It's real, Cal. It's real."

The words were spoken by Seth, his breath hot on his ear, but they were also *written.*

Not just words, either, but images. Images of smooth metal tunnels, spiraling from a center point outward like spokes on a wheel.

And the tanks; large tanks, *huge* tanks, that ran floor to ceiling. Inside one of them was a man, a man with tubes covering his nose and mouth. Bubbles rose to the surface of the tank, and his eyes were wide. There was a nameplate below the tank, inscribed with a name that Cal didn't recognize: C. Lawrence.

He swallowed hard, trying to make sense of what had happened. Never much of an artist, Cal had somehow managed to fill the pages with hundreds of these renderings, all the while with Seth breathing on his ear.

The air in the library stirred as he scribbled furiously, but nothing else seemed to change. Hours had passed, days, maybe, or maybe no time at all.

The pencil, reduced to a small nub not more than three inches long, rolled from his fingers and onto the table.

"What the hell?" he whispered.

His eyelids fluttered, and he sagged in his chair, overcome with exhaustion. But Seth reached out and grabbed him by the shoulders. With his touch came the briny smell of seawater, as if a wave had crashed at his feet.

"I told you," Seth said softly. "Mooreshead is a special place. It's a place where you can write your story."

Cal felt another bout of nausea, but Seth released his shoulders and it passed. With a cramped hand, he reached out and slammed the book closed.

There's only one last thing to do...

With a hand stricken by palsy, he grabbed the pencil and scribbled his name on the cover: *Callum Godfrey.*

Strangely disgusted by himself, Cal threw the pencil down for the final time. Whatever trickery was going on, he no longer wanted a part of it.

"I have to go," he whispered. He half-expected Seth to wrap his arms around him, perhaps even forcefully keep him here in the library. But the man didn't object.

"Cal, the stories are in your head—you *know* them. And the story of Mayor Partridge and Father McCabe is true. There is something in The Pit, a doorway—*The* Leporidae *burrow is long and deep*—and not all doors lead to the Marrow."

Cal was breathing heavily and his legs felt barely strong enough to hold him up.

The Marrow? What the hell is the Marrow?

"Pick up your book, Cal."

Cal did as he was instructed, but refused to look at the cover. Then Seth led him over to the shelf where he had first pulled the then empty book from.

"Put it back."

Cal, his brain still foggy, squatted and went to slide the green book back in the empty spot. But before he did, his eyes fell on another book. One with a worn leather cover and the words *Inter vivos et mortuos.*

Intrigued, he reached for this book, intent on pulling it out, but Seth stayed his hand.

"That's someone else's story, Cal. Not yours."

Cal nodded and slid the green book in beside the other.

Then he stood and turned to Seth, who was smiling again.

"One day you will make your own sacrifice—like the men in Askergan, the women in Stumphole Swamp."

Cal nodded and allowed Seth to guide him to the door.

It'll all be over soon. This queer dream will be over and I'll forget all about it.

Seth opened the door, and Cal squinted into the bright light. He was about to step outside, when Seth spoke again, drawing him back.

"Remember, Cal," he said, bringing a finger to his temple. "The story is in here."

Cal nodded a final time, then stepped out into the sun, far more confused than when he had arrived asking questions about a feud between Mooreshead's Mayor and a priest.

He left peering down into the eternal depths of the *Leporidae* burrow.

***

Cal waited outside Hank's house until the sun blinked out like a reptilian eye, with the cover of dusk as the first, transparent lid, followed by the imminent darkness brought on full-thickness skin flap.

The weather had cooled over the course of the last few hours, and there was the scent of impending rain in the air.

Little of this registered with Cal, however. His mind was still racing, his thoughts a runaway locomotive, replete with ideas and notions and ultimately confusion.

He had seen things today, things that couldn't possibly be real. He had written and drawn things that he had no business creating.

A spiral of tunnels, like spokes on a wheel… not all lead to the Marrow.

He had to tell Hank; he was compelled to tell his grinning friend about what he had a seen, and what the Curator had told him: the story of the priest and the mayor was true.

The priest made a sacrifice, and one day you will too.

But Cal had to wait. Hank's parents were strict and had rules against visitors on school nights. Which was ironic, given that like him, his friend rarely attended the institution.

Cal waited in the bushes across the street, aware that his own parents must be worried sick about him, but accepting of the consequences. This was more important.

This was *exciting*.

At half-past nine, the upstairs lights blinked out. Cal waited another five minutes, and a single light flicked on in the room on the left-hand side of the house.

Hank's room.

Reading, maybe?

But Hank wasn't much of a reader. A story-teller, sure, but not a reader.

Cal's brow furrowed just as the first drop of rain landed on his forehead. He wiped it away, realizing that it wasn't just wet with rain.

He was sweating, too.

The light blinked out again, and Cal's confusion deepened. When it turned on a second time, he wondered if perhaps Hank had spotted him earlier in the evening and was sending him a signal.

Cal shrugged and stepped out from the line of hedges. There was a street lamp off to his left, illuminating the quiet street in an ashen glow. He took two steps to his right, staying low, careful to stay out of the light in case Hank's parents were still awake.

Then he strode across the narrow berm and onto the street. As his shoes hit tarmac, a pitter-patter sound distracted him and he slunk back into the shadows. Cal's first thought was that it was just the rain picking up in intensity. But while a skyward glance confirmed that this was true, it wasn't the rain that he heard, but footsteps.

And then he saw her. Her blond hair was tied in a tight ponytail, and a smack of bright red lipstick stood out on her pale features like some sort of beacon.

But it was her eyes that gave it away. Stacey's green eyes were beaming as she made her way quickly across the street, then onto the lawn.

Cal's heart was racing in his chest.

No, come on. It can't be.

But it *was*.

The sound of a latch lifting echoed in the night, and the window with the light on opened about six inches.

Hank's bird-like nose peaked out.

"Stace?" he whispered. "They're asleep, come on up."

As Stacey made her way onto the lawn, then put her right foot in the trellis on the lower half of the porch, Cal remained frozen.

No, no way.

He recalled what Hank had said to him as he watched Stacey walk away from The Pit with Brent. He had felt a small tinge of jealousy then, but that was silly.

After all, Brent and Stacey were cousins.

You like her, don't you? Well, she likes you too, Cal. We can all see it.

Bullshit—all of it was bullshit. Hank had just been placating him so that he could get with her.

Calm down, Cal. There might be a rational explanation for all this. Homework, maybe? Group assignment?

Except that wasn't quite right; he knew that Brent and Hank had spent the day at The Pit.

Cal ground his teeth and felt his face tingle with heat. The rain that splashed down on him seemed to sizzle and boil upon touching his skin.

"Fucking Hank," he grumbled. "Fucking Hank!"

The words that came out of his mouth did so from between clenched teeth. And yet Hank, who was on high alert for his parents waking, heard the sound and he raised his head. Even Stacey, who was halfway up the side of the porch turned toward him.

Cal slunk into the shadows, trying to become one with the shrubbery.

Please don't see me. Please don't—

"Who's there?" Hank hissed. The rain was coming down harder now, making it difficult for Cal to make out the words.

How the fuck did they hear me?

He tried to remain completely still, going as far as to even hold his breath.

Stacey and Hank remained frozen as well, until Cal heard his friend's voice cut through the rain.

"Cal? Cal, is that you?"

Cal wasn't sure if it was Hank or Stacey who said the words, but it didn't matter. His reaction was visceral and immediate.

Cal started to run. With the rain pouring down on him, soaking his shoes and causing an accompanying splash with every footfall, Cal ran as fast as he could, trying his best to ignore his friends' shouts following him up the street.

Chapter 12

CAL HADN'T PLANNED ON coming to The Pit, but he wasn't surprised that that was where he ended up anyway.

The rain was nearing torrential status now, and the muddy, worn path that Cal took to the rim of the gravel pit was nearly impassable. Feet spread wide, he tried to avoid getting his shoes stuck, opting instead for the wet grass that flanked the path like sideburns.

He couldn't believe it. Hank had fucking lied to him, coerced him, tricked him so that he could get with Stacey.

It made no sense; why would Stacey pick Hank over him? Sure, he was big-boned, but Hank was a pimply-faced bespectacled whiny little bastard.

"Fuck," he swore. As he neared the edge of the gravel pit, approaching the area where they had sat the day prior, he suddenly regretted his decision to come here. Like a virus proliferating in his brain, this regret started to replicate, until it quickly got to the point where he regretted everything that had happened over the past few days.

The story that Hank had told him was obvious bullshit, obfuscating the truth in a lame attempt to keep him here in Mooreshead.

Yeah, Cal thought, *that's what this is all about, keeping me here.*

They all—Hank, Brent, Stacey—knew about his plans to get out of this boring, shit ass town and leave them behind. That's what pissed him off—it must be.

And his encounter with Seth Parsons? That was just a weird trick... Hank had put something in the whiskey. Like that blue/green alcohol... Absinthe, was that it? Yeah, he heard that that stuff can make you pretty twisted, give you hallucinations and shit. Or maybe the meeting had been less sinister, maybe it was just the result of his hangover mixed with toxic mold spores or some shit.

Cal rubbed his sore wrist absently.

"Fucking lies, fucking bullshit lies," he turned his head to the heavens, blinking at that rain that pelted down on his face. "All of it, this whole place is just a bunch of boring fucking lies!"

"Cal?"

Cal's heart leaped into his throat, and he spun on his heels. He moved onto the muddy path as he did, and his feet immediately sunk several inches into the muck.

Hank was standing in his soaking wet t-shirt, his hands held out in front of him, palms up. Stacey stood behind him, her blond hair hanging in wet strings in front of her face.

"What the fuck do you want?" Cal snarled. "I thought you were my friend!"

Hank's hawkish features twisted into a grimace.

"I am your friend! I—"

"You what? You just lied to me so that you could fuck her?" he demanded, lifting his chin to Stacey as he spoke.

Stacey's eyes went wide, and Cal had to shout to be heard over the torrential downpour.

"Oh, yeah, what are you going to say? You're going to say that you weren't fucking? That you weren't doing that shit behind my back?"

Stacey's expression changed from shock to sheer rage. She moved forward and tried to push by Hank, but he moved with her, remaining firmly planted between them.

"Are you fucking serious?" she shouted, her voice shrill. "What gives you the right? I can do whatever the hell I want. I don't owe you anything. We're just friends, Cal. I'm not sure what you thought... *why* you thought that we had something going on, but we didn't and we don't. So, stop being a fucking baby and let's go home."

The words struck Cal like a flurry of punches and he took a few steps backward, his feet slurping loudly in the mud.

"Well—"

A loud crack of lightning split the sky, illuminating their faces. Cal ducked instinctively, and then straightened, feeling embarrassed for more reason than one.

"I—I just... I just thought that—"

A massive, rolling wave of thunder interrupted his blubbering. Cal felt his chest flutter with the change in pressure, then instinctively glanced over his shoulder and stared into the gravel pit.

The Leporidae *burrow is long and deep...*

It seemed to him that the thunder hadn't so much as echoed in The Pit as it had originated from there. There was already a pool of water at the bottom, one that sloshed and churned with—

"No, fuck you, Cal. You have no right. There was nothing ever between us, and you wanna know why?"

Cal's head whipped around again, but this time he said nothing.

"Easy, Stacey," Hank offered, but Stacey was having none of it.

"No, fuck this. Someone has to say it... it's because you are fucking obsessed with everything being so boring, and thinking that you are," she threw her arms up dramatically, "*for some reason* better than everyone. You think you're too good for Hank, for Brent, for me. Too good for all of fucking Mooreshead."

Cal was so shocked at this sudden outburst that he couldn't even formulate a response.

"But the truth is—"

"Stacey, please," Hank interrupted.

"—no, let me finish. The truth is—" now it was Stacey's turn to turn her head to the Heavens, before returning her gaze to Cal. "The truth is that *you* are boring, Cal. You are the most fucking boring person I've ver—"

"Stacey! Enough!" Hank shouted.

This time, she shut up.

Cal started to cry. He couldn't help it. The tears poured down his cheeks in rivulets that rivaled those that bled down into The Pit.

"Fuck," Hank whispered moving forward in the mud. "Cal, c'mon, man. She didn't mean it."

Cal turned sideways protectively as Hank continued to approach. Before he knew it, his old friend was directly beside him.

"Let's just—let's just go home," he said, reaching out and putting an arm around Cal.

Cal didn't mean to do what he did next. It was instinct, fueled by his anger, confusion, and just plain disgust. Disgust at himself, disgust at the fact that what Stacey had said about him had all been true.

"Don't fucking touch me," he whispered as he reached out and wrenched Hank's arm from his shoulder.

Under any other conditions, Hank would have just shrugged this off, righted himself, and they would have all been on their merry way. It probably wouldn't have raised an eyebrow. After all, Cal didn't like being touched.

Only these weren't normal conditions.

Hank's heels slipped in the mud and he stumbled forward. Had his shoes landed one foot to the left, they would have locked in the mud as Cal's were now. But Hank's sneakers came down too close to the lip of The Pit, and they slipped on the eroded edge.

Cal's mouth made a wide 'O' shape and he cried out as he reached for his friend.

"Noooo!" Hank screamed as he tumbled over the edge.

Chapter 13

THE SINGLE SYLLABLE DRONED on and on, radiating up the sides of the gravel pit.

It was Hank who shouted it—*noooo!*—but Cal and maybe Stacey too, had picked up the refrain.

Cal yanked his feet from the mud and moved cautiously toward the rim of The Pit, which had now acquired the consistency of runny oatmeal. He made it in time to see Hank still airborne—although this seemed impossible given the number of seconds it had taken him to reach the edge—his eyes and mouth wide.

Just as Cal's foot slipped off the edge, Hank's back struck the side of the embankment, and even with the rain pouring as it was, Cal heard the air forced from his lungs.

His friend's eyes rolled back, and then his entire body seemed to follow suit, and Cal found himself watching Hank tumbling head over heels, throwing up mud from every limb, picking up speed like a wayward snowball.

Cal tried to maintain his own footing, balancing his terror, enthusiasm and desperation on a grain of sand, while at the same time trying to avoid Hank's fate.

He shifted his feet sideways, strafing down the muddy surface quickly, but carefully. Hank was still spinning ahead of him at such a speed that Cal realized there was no way he would be able to catch him. Not until he hit the bottom, that is.

Anticipating this, Cal lifted his gaze, squinting heavily as he sought the endgame.

And then he saw it.

There was some kind of protrusion, something massive and gleaming, jutting from the side of the bowl, about three-quarters to the roiling cesspool at the bottom.

In all of his years of coming here, Cal had never seen any-thing embedded in the side of The Pit—anything but roots and weeds, that is—but the thick streams of water pouring down the sides had already caused major erosion.

The object appeared large and metal.

And Hank's listless body was tumbling right at it.

This time, it was only Cal who shouted.

"Hank!"

He reached out in futility—instinctively, really, as there was no chance he could reach Hank. All Cal could do was watch in horror as his friend's body flipped one final time, and then his back smashed against the metal object.

A jolt of thunder erupted at the moment of impact, giving the sound of Hank's cracking spine an ethereal, monstrous quality that made Cal's entire body shudder. Through tear- and rain-streaked vision, he saw Hank's eyelids peel back, his eyes bulge, and his mouth twist into a grimace.

Then he went still.

Completely still.

Cal careened after him, throwing caution to the wind. But before he could reach Hank, his body started to move again, not pin-wheeling in a cartoonish manner as it had before, but this time languidly, carried on the surface of the mud like a preg-nant raindrop.

Breathing heavily, his throat burning, Cal finally made it to his friend.

He dropped to his knees, driving them both into the mud as he wrapped his arms around Hank's waist, rooting them, fi-nally halting what had seemed like an infinite descent. Another liquid, something thicker than the rain that soaked him, coated Hank's entire back, and eventually Cal's hands as well.

He didn't need the weak illumination from the half-covered moon to reveal what it was.

He already knew.

Cal swallowed hard and looked back up the side of the gravel pit.

The metal object that Hank had struck was more clearly visible from below, and he finally realized what it was. It was the backhoe of a giant excavator, and one of the massive, metal prongs that extended from the bucket was covered in blood. The rain beat down on the backhoe, sending the blood streaming down the gleaming metal surface, where it eventually mixed with the rain that sluiced toward him. Cal's eyes followed the thin tendrils of dark liquid until they joined with the source.

"Hank!" Cal shouted, realizing that his friend's body had gone completely rigid, tetanic, even. He wanted to shake Hank, to wake them both up from this horrible, shared nightmare, but he was afraid of inflicting any more damage. "Please, Hank, wake up!"

Hank's eyelids fluttered, and then his eyes rolled forward almost mechanically, as if requiring great effort.

"I never... I never meant—" Hank croaked.

Cal sobbed.

"Shut up! It doesn't matter, Hank. Just shut up."

Hank's back suddenly tensed, and Cal felt more blood from the wound cover his arms.

"No, don't move! You can't move—you're bleeding."

Hank closed his eyes again, and he took a hitched breath.

"Cal, Stacey was wrong. You don't *think* you are better than us, better than Mooreshead, but you *are*. You're destined for greater things than this."

Cal ignored his friend's comment, and he quickly turned his eyes back up the slope.

Stacey...

Lightning struck then, a pitchfork schism of brilliance in the sky.

And that's when he saw her, staring at him with something akin to loathing, or fear, or both.

Or something else entirely.

"Stacey!" he yelled, his voice already hoarse from trying to be heard over the torrential downpour. "Go get help! *Please!*"

She remained frozen in place.

"Stacey!"

But she still didn't reply.

Hank sighed, and Cal turned back to him.

"No, no, no! Open your fucking eyes, Hank. You're not going anywhere."

And to his surprise, Hank listened to him.

Only his eyes were cloudy now, lacking the lucidity of even a moment ago.

Cal wiped the water from his face, but nothing changed; Hank's eyes *were* dark, the pupils enormous, inexplicably occupying all of the white.

And in the center of those pupils were flecks of sand, flecks that grew and grew and grew, until Cal realized he was staring at some sort of surf.

A surf... inside my friend's eyes... what is happening?

It struck him that whatever drugs or mold spores that had altered his mind back in the library must still be messing with his senses.

"This is not—" *possible*, he meant to say, but another voice cut him off mid-sentence.

"You have a story to write, Cal... an important story, more important than Mooreshead, although this is where it started, and this is the place you will return," someone whispered—*Hank, it had to be Hank, who else could it be?*—but Cal couldn't draw his gaze away from his friend's eyes to look at his mouth and lips to confirm.

And if it wasn't Hank, Cal wasn't sure he would be able to deal with the implications.

"Please," Cal whispered. "Oh, please, God, don't let him die."

But Hank and whatever Lord presided over The Pit pleaded ignorance or defiance and failed to intervene.

Hank's back arched once more, and then he fell completely still.

"No! *Plea*—"

But the words were cut from his throat as the sky suddenly opened and the sun—*my god it's near midnight, where did the sun come from*—beat down on Cal warming him in a way he never thought possible.

Chapter 14

EUPHORIA.

Cal drank every now and then in this very gravel pit with his friends and twice had tried smoking pot. But while these influences always left him with a sense of calm, a thankful reprieve from the constant flood of thoughts, he had never felt anything like this.

It was as if every one of his neurons had fired at once, budding neurotransmitters of Dopamine bridging every gap, every synapse. If he hadn't been a virgin, he might have compared the feeling to that very first orgasm.

For once in his entire life, Cal felt *complete*, whole.

And he also felt something else... a gentle tug on his very essence, teasing him not toward the sun that shone on him with near blinding fury, but toward the bottom of the gravel pit.

Like the allure of the sea, staring out over its infinite brilliance, calmed by its lulling and hypnotic surface, Cal felt a need to go down into the basin, which continued to froth and boil with unrepentant febrility.

The *Leporidae* burrow was right *there*, right beneath the pool of churning water that suddenly smelled more of salty brine than of silt-laden rain.

Cal's jaw went slack, and in that moment the sun blinked out again, and he was transported back to his present reality, his arms wrapped around his friend's dead body. At some point, he had lowered his head to Hank's chest.

You will make a sacrifice, they all do, Seth Parsons had said. *The* Leporidae *burrow is long and deep...*

Cal straightened and looked down at himself, curiously, as if what he was seeing was all new to him, as if this body wasn't the same one he had inhabited for the past fifteen plus years. He had ejaculated in his jeans, he realized with abject horror.

No matter how pleasurable the experience of a few moments ago had been, he was now overcome with a sense of foreboding.

And guilt.

Still crying, he tried to push himself to his feet, but found himself unable. His knees had sunk deep into the thick mud as he had cradled his friend, and now it reached almost to his crotch.

Cal grunted as he drove his fists downward, but this only served to bury his hands and wrists in the mud.

In that moment, the sky opened up, and it seemed to Cal as if an entire ocean was spilling down on him now, sending a deluge into the basin as if it were the lowest point on Earth.

Cal started to scream, and he scanned the ridge where he had seen Stacey standing only moments ago.

Only she wasn't there anymore.

His eyes whipped all the way around the perimeter of The Pit, moving so quickly that he felt dizzy.

"Stacey! *Stacey!*" he shouted.

It was no use. Thunder seemed to coincide with every time he opened his mouth, drowning his words with their celestial bravado.

The water flow was so strong that in moments, not only was Cal still sinking, but he was moving, too, sliding toward the trough basin.

"Fuck!" he swore, still holding onto Hank's arm with his left hand. He somehow managed to turn his body so that he was facing out of The Pit, and he grasped the mud, intending on pulling both of them toward the surface.

His fingers closed on nothing but water.

Cal slipped onto his stomach and water splashed his face, causing him to sputter. The flow was so powerful that it tried to force his head down, to push it into the mud, to drown him.

He wouldn't let it.

Cal drove his neck up, finally breaking the surface.

A quick glance showed that he had slipped closer to the bottom of The Pit, with Hank leading the way.

"I won't let you go!" he cried. "Hank, I won't fucking let you go!"

Hank's body was mostly covered in water now, and while he appeared to be floating, no matter how hard Cal tugged, he wouldn't budge.

It was as if something was holding Hank there, and Cal too, rooting them in place.

Something that desperately wanted them — *needed* them — to enter to the simmering basin.

Cal swallowed hard and tried to claw his way out of the gravel pit.

It was no use. With one hand on Hank, he just kept slipping lower.

Hank was dragging him down.

Sobbing uncontrollably now, he turned back to the pool, which was only six or eight feet from Hank's head.

Even though water was pouring down the slopes from all sides in thick torrents, the pool was frothing more than it should be.

More than was natural.

And then Cal saw it.

A hand, black as tar, broke the surface. Only the fingertips at first, which was why Cal's initial instinct was that it was only some other discarded machinery that had been long buried.

But when he saw the familiar shape of a palm, and then a wrist, he knew that this was no machine.

When a second hand broke the surface, and then a third, followed quickly by others, so many that he couldn't count, all desperately grasping at the air, Cal knew that this was no illusion.

And he also knew what happened to those workers, all those years ago.

"No, please," he sobbed. "Oh, please, God, save me."

But there was no God; or if there was one, he wasn't here, he wasn't in The Pit.

And he wasn't listening.

There was only Cal and his story, which now included Hank's dead body.

He tried once more to yank Hank up the slope, but his efforts were futile.

One of the grasping hands finally grabbed hold of Hank's hair, and it pulled.

The yank was fierce, dragging Hank's entire face and shoulders beneath the water, which caused Cal, who was still holding his friend's arm, to slip in the mud.

After feeling his knees slide, an idea, a horrible, terrible idea, formed in his mind.

Hank's head resurfaced, his black eyes still wide.

"I'm so sorry," he whispered as a second hand, this time wrapping itself around Hank's nose and mouth, joined the first.

Cal waited, and when they yanked again, he allowed himself to be pulled with it. The top half of Hank's body was dragged beneath the water, and just when Cal felt the pull relent, he planted his foot on Hank's hip and pushed.

He hesitated just long enough to see his friend's body completely submerge, leaving in its wake a series of small bubbles.

And that was it.

Hank Harper, his best friend, had been reduced to a memory and a series of bubbles in less than the time it took to tie a shoelace.

Cal shouted once more, something unintelligible this time, and then turned his back on the rabbit hole.

He started to scramble up the side of The Pit, fighting both water and temptation until he eventually made it to the top.

Chapter 15

CAL SLAMMED THE HEEL of his hand against the large wooden door.

"Open the door!" he yelled at the top of his lungs as he pounded. "Open the fucking door!"

Thunder rolled and Cal turned his head skyward as he continued to thump until his hands went numb. Rain filled his eyes, and he closed them, and then spat it from his mouth.

He saw Hank's face, his black eyes, then remembered the fleeting euphoria.

What happened down there? What the fuck just happened?

Hank's own words whispered in his mind: *A passage to Hell, Cal. They say that the men had unearthed a passage to Hell.*

There was a click, and the next time his fist moved forward, he stumbled with it.

"H-h-hello?" a woman stuttered, sliding out of the way to avoid Cal as he careened through the doorway.

"We're closed, sir!"

Cal regained his footing and then blinked the tears and rain from his eyes. When they finally focused, he found himself staring at a woman in her late sixties, her face etched with thick lines. She had brown hair that was pulled into a ponytail that was so tight it gave her paper-thin eyebrows a perpetual optimistic expression, which was very likely her intention.

"What?" Cal stammered, trying hard to catch his breath. "Where is he? Where's Seth?"

The woman eyed him suspiciously.

"Are you on some sort of drugs?"

"What? No! What are you talking about?" Cal grit his teeth, trying to bury his frustration. "Where's Seth? I need to talk to Seth! He needs to tell me where they took him."

The woman, clearly concerned now, took a small step backward.

"Listen, I'm not sure what's going on here, or what you're on, but my second cousin is friends with the Sheriff. I think you should get out of here and sober up before I give him a call."

Cal felt his face go red. After all that had happened, he couldn't believe that this woman was doing this to him now. He reached out and grabbed her by the shoulders.

"Tell me where Seth is! I need to talk to him!"

The woman's eyes went wide.

"You're hurting me," she whispered and Cal, finally realizing what he was doing let go and backed away. When he spoke again, his voice was quieter, but the intensity of his words didn't change.

"Seth Parsons... I need to speak to him. Please, if he's here, I need to speak to him right away."

The woman wasn't bothering to hide her fear now and moved closer to the desk at the back of the room as she spoke.

"I don't know a Seth Parsons. Never heard of him."

"What? He was here earlier."

The woman was nearly at the desk now.

"Is he... a student, like you?"

Cal shook his head and looked around the room. It was as hazy as it had been earlier, and just as empty.

Where the fuck is he?

"No, not a student. He's the... the..." he racked his mind, trying to come up with the word that Seth had used.

Cultivator? Cremator? What the fuck is it?

And then it came to him.

"The Curator!" he exclaimed. "He's the Curator!"

Cal was expecting recognition to flash over the woman's features and was sorely disappointed when none came.

She had no idea who or what he was talking about.

Cal strode forward, and the woman cowered. His shame was only outweighed by his confusion and frustration.

But the librarian wasn't his target. Instead, he went toward the door off to the left, the one that Seth had emerged from after taking a piss.

Only, there was no door; at least not one that Cal could see.

"What the fuck is going on?" he whispered, running his pruned fingertips across the wall, searching for a seam. "Where's the fucking door? Where's the bathroom?"

Somewhere behind him, he heard the woman rise and scramble toward the telephone on the desk.

Cal didn't pay her any mind.

Tears were filling his vision now, threatening to spill over.

"Where are you?"

A few more desperate seconds of searching and Cal gave up. With renewed determination, he moved away from the wall, and instead focused on the bookcase. Someone had moved the ladder since Cal had been there earlier in the day, and now it was blocking the area he had leaned down and placed the book with the green cover.

His book.

Cal shoved the ladder out of the way, the wheels whirring on the track as it slid along the rail.

Then he dropped to his hands and knees and started to scan the lowest row of books. He ran his fingers over their bindings, searching for a particular spine.

But, like his search for the door, he came up empty.

"What the fuck is going on here?" he said softly. A sudden sharp pain erupted behind his eyes, and he squeezed them tightly, gritting his teeth.

Cal collapsed to a seated position and tried to slow his racing heart by taking several deep breaths.

It didn't help.

Every breath reminded him of Hank's last, when his body had tensed, then finally gone slack.

And Hank's image reminded him of the euphoria, of the sun beating down on him, his ejaculation.

And from that moment onward, he knew that any pleasure he may experience would be forever linked to pain, to that instant of loss.

Cal's eyes snapped open, and he saw red.

He grabbed the first book he saw and ripped it off the shelf, tossing it behind him. Then he grabbed the next and threw it as well.

Then the next, and the next after that.

In less than a minute, Cal had torn out the entire row of books, at least fifty, maybe more, and had littered them behind him as if preparing for his version of the Bonfire of the Vanities.

"Where the fuck is it!" he screamed. And then, with every word, he pulled out another book and tossed it into the pile with the others. "Where—the—fuck—is—it?"

Only then did he realize that he could hear the faint, yet distinct sound of sirens coming from somewhere outside.

Cal stopped pulling out books and stood. Every one of his movements now was slow, labored, as if someone had sucked the library air out and replaced it with a thin taffy.

He turned to the woman, who was now huddling below the desk, the phone still clutched to her ear.

She didn't even look up at him.

"I'm sorry," he said softly. "I'm so sorry."

There was no specific target for this apology, although there could have been many.

The librarian.

Stacey.

Brent.

His parents.

And, of course, Hank.

Cal staggered toward the door. When his hands smashed against it, it flung open with greater ease than its size would suggest possible.

A second later, he was outside in the rain again, and a second after that, he was on the run, putting Mooreshead behind him as fast as he possibly could.

Callum Godfrey was desperate for excitement in his life, but he had never dreamed that it would come like this.

Mooreshead, which was boring with a capital B, had suddenly changed into something worse.

Something much, much worse.

PART II- Sight of the Marrow

Chapter 16

PRESENT DAY

ROBERT WATTS KNEW HE was dreaming, but for some reason, this didn't seem to matter to him. It *should* have mattered, it should have mattered a great deal, but it didn't.

Maybe dreams are part of the Marrow, too... remnants of the quiddity of others... of the Sea, he thought absently. *Maybe there are hints in these dreams, hints to make this all go away. To go back to how things were before...*

There was a man on the bed, lying on his back, the pale bottoms of his feet pointed towards Robert. Just above the man's knees, his gaze was drawn upward, following another body now, one with smooth, bare buttocks, and an arched back.

It was a back he recognized well. His eyes continued upward, passing her smooth shoulder blades, and then the gentle curve of her neck. The woman's dark hair was twisted to one side, cascading over the front of one shoulder and out of sight.

She was rocking rhythmically, sliding back and forth on the man with the pale feet, who all the while remained deathly still.

Robert found that not only could he see in this dream, but he could hear as well; he could hear the soft sound of a woman moaning, the mews coinciding with every shift of her hips.

Wendy, he thought, a pang of guilt and anger striking him simultaneously in the solar plexus.

"Faster," a man husked. "Faster, faster, *faster!*"

Robert swallowed hard and somehow managed to turn his ethereal form so that he could observe from the couple from one side. He didn't really want to see—he felt like a voyeur— but Robert knew that he *had* to see.

His eyes fell on the swell of the woman's stomach, but thankfully their genitals were mashed together, sparing him that sight at least. He saw the roundness of her breasts, surprisingly full despite her thin frame, sweat beading on the top, her nipples, rosy and pink, standing erect. The man reached behind her, and his hands, hairy, just like his calves and shins, gripped her buttocks, grinding her body into his.

A sob escaped him then, and the rhythmic coitus suddenly stopped.

"Did you hear that?" the man whispered.

"No," the woman replied flatly. "Keep going."

"I heard something," the man raised his head, and Robert felt his entire being flush with anger.

It was Landon; it was Landon fucking Underhill, his one-time boss back when he worked at Audex Accounting.

He was sweating, and his mouth, nearly hidden in his thick, brown beard, was closed tightly.

"No, seriously, I heard—"

The woman turned then, and her eyes fell directly on Robert. His heart, previously thumping away in his chest, stopped beating altogether.

It wasn't Wendy.

It was her body; Lord knows he had spent more than enough time with that body, especially in their earlier years, but it wasn't her face.

Robert felt like he was going to be sick.

The face that stared back at him had huge, black orbs for eyes, their protuberance so pronounced that they seemed lidless. She had no nose; in its place was a hole in the center of her face. Air puffed in and out of that bastardized orifice, and Robert realized with growing horror that what he had mistaken as manifestations of heightened ecstasy was simply air chuffing in and out of the hole like an unbridled steam engine.

Maggots writhed in and out of the rotting flesh on her face, making tracks not unlike stitches inserted by an amateur surgeon.

It was Jacky Sommers, the golden-haired beauty from the Harlop Estate, the one who so long ago he had had a tryst with in the mud.

"What are you doing here?" the rotting corpse hissed. The sound was whistly and horrible, coming not just from behind the lipless mouth, but from the hole that was her nose, and the tear in her cheek. "You shouldn't be here!"

Robert tried to back out of the dream, to direct his body, his mind, elsewhere, but found that he could not.

When the woman placed her bony fingers on the mattress and slipped off Landon, who was grinning now, a thin line in his beard that spread from ear to ear, Robert tried to scream, but once again found himself unable.

Jacky started to slide toward him on all fours, her breasts now blue and veiny and sagging nearly to the floor.

"You shouldn't be here," she said again in that horrible voice.

She was nearly upon him now. With every inch that she crawled forward, the flesh on her arms seemed to decay by a week, a month, a *year*, the skin taking on first bluish then green then black hues.

It fell away in putrid clumps.

Someone—Landon—was laughing, a horrible, deep rumbling sound that made Robert's head pulse and blurred his vision.

And then Jacky was directly in front of him, reeking of rot and decay.

It was only then that Robert realized that he had a body in this dream world—*his* body—and he was completely naked.

But like before, it felt like an organic shell, simply a vessel for his mind, and whatever connection had once bound the two had been broken, snapped and tossed aside like kindling.

He couldn't move, couldn't even raise a finger let alone back away.

The woman, the beast, the abomination reared back and pushed her horrible breasts into his face.

He gagged, but like most of his visceral functions, he was unable to even vomit.

A horrible, snaked tongue flicked out of her lipless mouth in a strangely provocative gesture and he was disgusted to discover that he felt a familiar tightening between his legs.

The thing that had once been Jacky Sommers leaned back and her bony, skeletal hand snaked out and squeezed the meat between his legs.

"No," he moaned, surprised that he could actually get the word out.

"Oh, yes, Robert Watts. Oh, yes," the thing hissed.

And then it was on top of him, straddling his lower body as it had done with Landon seconds ago.

Robert wanted nothing more than to be out of there, to be free of this horrible nightmare, irrespective of whatever hints or clues that it was trying to tell, but the traction in this reality was simply too strong.

The second he entered Jacky's corpse, he felt his loins tighten and a familiar tingling sensation built in his scrotum.

Robert ejaculated immediately, and even though it was horrible—the sight, the smell, the simple *idea*—the pleasure was immense, and a long, rolling moan exited his mouth.

For a brief second, his eyes closed.

A waft of putrefaction hit him in the face, and he opened them again.

The beast, Jacky Sommers, or Wendy, or whatever it was, was gone. In its place was Shelly, her belly huge and round and distended.

She was on her back and appeared to be sleeping, and Robert, confused, glanced down at his own body, fearing that he would still be naked, his prick covered in decomposing flesh.

But he wasn't naked; he was wearing shorts.

What's happening to me? His mind wailed. *What's happening?*

His eyes flicked to Shelly's belly again, and for a moment he saw movement within. At first, it was simple, indistinct pressure, but as the shadow traveled across her belly, *within* her belly, Robert realized that it had acquired a form he recognized.

The object moved back and forth as if the fetus were waving, and then it stopped in the center.

It started to push, and to Robert's horror, he made out three distinct impressions.

Talons.

Talons that matched the marks on his leg, the ones had been seared into his flesh when Leland, his father, had touched him.

And then Shelly screamed.

Robert tried to cover his ears, to block out her wails, but his body failed to comply. It wouldn't have mattered anyway.

The sound was all around him, in him.

And there was something else, too. The laughter, laughter that he had first mistaken as Landon's, had returned.

Only it wasn't Landon's.

It was Leland's.

"The baby's coming, Robert," a male voice echoed in his head, cutting through the high-pitch drone of Shelly's agonized cries. "The baby's coming very soon, and when it does, we're going to be a family again."

Chapter 17

CAL STARED DOWN AT his friend's feverish, clenched body, as Robert's eyes rolled back in his head.

"Should we wake him?" he asked quietly.

Chloe Black, who had since rid herself of the cloak and thus the moniker of the same name, shook her head.

"No," she said in her gravelly voice. "He needs to sleep. Please, just let him sleep."

Cal continued to watch his friend, trying desperately, and failing to understand what he must be going through. Sure, Cal had a tortured past, but nothing like Robert's.

Robert had lost his wife, his daughter. He had stared into the eyes of pure evil, faced his very own soul.

He had found another woman, and lost her too.

And now this.

His unborn daughter taken from him, reduced to a pawn in Satan's mad game.

Robert's cheek twitched and Cal resisted the urge to wrap his arms around him, to hold him tight, as he had once done with Hank Harper.

"What—" he cleared his throat. "What's happening to him?"

"He's had a break… his mind has shattered, and it's trying to heal itself."

Chloe's answer had been so quick, and sounded so clinical, that it drew his gaze.

He found it difficult to look directly at the woman, and it wasn't only because her face looked like the whipped hide of a rented mule. It was something else, there was something secretive buried in that scarred face.

And he was sick of secrets.

Secrets—Rob's and Sean's, Shelly's—were what led them to this place, to this time.

"How can you know?"

Chloe looked away and Cal followed her gaze toward the water overlooking the embankment. It was much like the way he envisioned the Marrow, all frothing and churning, a torrid mix of dissension and confusion.

Only it wasn't the Marrow. It was either the New York Harbor or the Atlantic Ocean, or something else entirely.

They had walked so far, for so long, first in the tunnels leading away from Sacred Heart Orphanage, and then along the rocky terrain, and eventually leading to this beach, that he wasn't completely sure where he was anymore.

"I know," Chloe began slowly. "Because I saw it happen to someone before."

Cal's gaze moved to the back of her head, to the scared ribbons that made up her scalp.

Her life had been torn to pieces as well; quite literally. Her family was destroyed, both of her sons entwined in a death match of the sort that he could have never imagined before all of this had started.

Aiden stepped forward and asked the question that was bouncing around in Cal's brain.

"Who? Who did this happen to before?"

Chloe hesitated, and when Cal reached out and brushed the back of her arm, she recoiled.

"Leland," she said flatly. "It happened to Leland."

Cal froze, and he heard either Agent Cherry or Detective Hugh exhale loudly behind him.

Leland? This happened to Leland?

An image of the thing that had pulled itself out of the portal in Sean's chest, a massive, winged thing with iron hooves flashed in his mind and he involuntarily shuddered.

It was hard for Cal to imagine Leland as anything remotely human, let alone something that resembled, either in form or spirit, his friend who lay collapsed on the ground by his feet.

The sound of a buzzing telephone broke the uncomfortable silence, and Cal finally pulled his eyes away from Chloe and the water.

Agent Cherry, his face a mess of bruises and dark smudges, pulled a phone from his pocket. The man's lips were dry, and Cal knew what he was even though they had yet to share more than a dozen words.

He could see it in his face.

He was an addict, and the man was hurting for his next fix. If Cal had been forced to guess, he would have picked alcohol as his drug of choice.

Cherry's eyes dropped to the phone, and then, seeing a number he recognized, he cleared his throat and answered.

"Agent Cherry."

There was a short pause, during which his gaze lifted. All five sets of eyes were on him, but he seemed unfazed by this.

"Yes. There has been a… some sort of…"

Agent Cherry paused to listen.

"Yes, of course. I understand."

He pulled the phone away from his ear, a queer expression on his face. Instead of putting it back into his pocket, he held it out to Chloe.

"It's FBI Director Ames, and he wants to speak to you."

Cal was initially taken aback by this, but then he remembered something that Chloe had said in the car, back when he had known her only as the Cloak.

There are people in high places that know about this... that might be able to help.

The woman's small, scarred hand reached out and took the phone, and then she turned her back to them.

"Yes?" There was a pause, and then Chloe said, "Yes, but we need helicopter evac."

And then she went silent.

Cal waited for almost a minute, before Chloe pulled the phone from her head and hung up without uttering another word.

She handed it back to Agent Cherry.

Then, for what felt like the hundredth time, Chloe turned to stare at the water. Cal felt another pang of sadness for the disfigured woman.

"Brett and Hugh, you have other business to attend to, I believe?"

Cal drew a sharp breath and his eyebrows knitted.

"What? You can't leave us—"

Chloe silenced him by raising a finger.

"Brett..."

The man closed his sunken eyes and became so still that Cal thought that he had fallen asleep standing up. Hugh, a confused expression on his young face, reached out to touch the other man, but before his fingers brushed his arm, Brett's lids opened.

"Yes; we need to go." He turned to Hugh, who was staring at him expectantly. "I need your help, Hugh. FBI Director Ames has asked if you would come with me."

Hugh's light-colored eyebrows lifted.

"Where?" he asked in a small voice.

Cal observed the scene with incredulity. To his knowledge, the men had only just met and yet Hugh already seemed subservient to him, FBI Agent or not. Back in the orphanage, Cal had seen the way that Hugh looked at the other, older detective, the one who had been killed by Bella and sent to the Marrow.

Hugh looked up at the man. And now that he was gone... well, Hugh was left wanting.

Cal didn't blame him. The same thing had happened when he had first fled Mooreshead, after Hank...

He pushed the thoughts from his mind.

"We're going south," Brett replied with a sigh. "There is something that I need to finish. Something evil, something that took my... my partner, Kendra." He lowered his voice an octave. "My Ken-Ken."

The name sounded strangely familiar to Cal, but he couldn't place it. It seemed to him that there were fibers in this world — tiny, invisible threads — that connected everything back to the Marrow.

And for all he knew, to other worlds as well.

It was all connected... it was all a story to tell.

His story.

"Okay," was Hugh's only response.

The two men then turned to Cal and Chloe, and then to Aiden, who hung respectively four or five feet behind them at all times.

"We will return — before this is all over, Hugh and I will come back and help finish this... finish this *thing*," Brett promised.

Despite the man's obvious problems — *alcohol, he's an alcoholic* — for some reason Cal knew that this was a promise that would only be broken if his quiddity was sent to the Marrow.

"You can't—we need—I—*ahhh*," Cal stammered. It was a lost cause. These men were off to fulfill another duty, another story. He shook his head in disgust, displeasure, anguish.

"We'll be back," Brett repeated, and with a final nod to Aiden, they turned on their heels and started away.

South...

South seemed a far way to go. Too far, maybe.

Cal watched them leave, his head low, his shoulders slumped.

"It's time," Chloe whispered from behind him.

Cal replied without turning, his eyes still focused on the two men's fading silhouettes.

"Time for what?"

Her answer chilled his blood, bringing back a flood of memories from his teenage years, memories that he had locked away.

"Time to see the Curator, Cal."

Chapter 18

"WE NEED TO KEEP moving," Chloe said.

Cal grunted, and adjusted his grip on the pieces of driftwood that he and Agent Cherry had fashioned into a makeshift travois before the man had left. The four of them, including Aiden, were making their way down the beach, putting as much distance between them and the orphanage as possible.

But it was slow going. The sand was heavy and wet, and Cal was struggling to pull Robert's body, despite the changes that his own had undergone over the past few months.

The Curator.

His initial response had been one of shock, then disbelief crept in.

It couldn't be the same man. It couldn't be... what was his name? Stuart? Steven? Seth?

Yes, that was it, *Seth.*

He saw a flash of long blond hair, of the California accent, if he could place it as such. An idea of California, anyway.

Seth Parsons.

No, it couldn't be that man, the same man in the library. The one with the strange book.

His book, full of strange architectural drawings of tunnels and tanks and other things that he had no business knowing let alone reproducing.

Cal shook his head and strode forward.

That was a dream, a drug-induced hallucination. Nothing more.

"How much farther?" he asked as he stared at the expanse of gray beach. Only Chloe seemed to know exactly where they were going, and even that had come into doubt after the third or fourth hour of trudging in the sand.

Night had descended on them like a cloud of bats, and now they only had stars to illuminate their way. A quick glance over his shoulder revealed that the orphanage had long melted into the dark horizon. Even the giant whirlwind spire of light and fury that had extended to the heavens was no longer visible.

"Can we stop?" he offered when there was no response to his initial query.

His hands were blistered, and his legs were numb from walking for so long — walking and pulling... and pulling and walking.

His feet were a mess, his running shoes sloppy from the wet sand.

Cal briefly wondered if trench foot was possible in less than one day. If it was, he had, of that he was certain.

To his surprise, Chloe stopped cold in front of him, and he nearly rammed into her from behind.

"We can stay here for the night," she said softly.

Cal looked around. The beach seemed endless, extending forever in both directions. As he stared, the clouds that cloaked the moon moved on to other business, providing them with some much-needed illumination. The blue light reflected off the body of water, which had since calmed almost to the point of ice.

But beneath the surface, it was anything but still; it teemed with life. Phosphorescent jellyfish drifted toward the surface in a hypnotic, neon dance, before plunging back down into the depths. Schools of herring formed distinct, direct paths like the ocean's very own blood vessels. In the distance, Cal heard the splash of what might have been a whale's great tail slapping at the otherwise unbroken demeanor.

"Here?" he asked, a tremor in his voice. He didn't like being in the open, especially with that horrible winged thing so close. "Aren't you worried about Leland? The Goat?"

Chloe shook her head.

"No, we're far enough away now. He won't bother us here. Besides, he has what he needs."

An image of Shelly, her face the epitome of terror, her hands clutching her swollen middle, flooded his mind and he shuddered.

She wasn't his—he had wanted her to be, surely—but she wasn't. She was Robert's, and yet he still felt guilt at having left her. After all, she was his friend. And the last time that a woman had come between himself and a friend, things had ended badly for everyone.

Very badly.

As if reading his mind, Chloe said, "We can't get her back. Only Robert can do that now."

Cal groaned and lowered the travois gently to the ground. After confirming that Robert was still asleep, if that's really what he was doing, Cal stretched his back and legs, trying to work out some of the soreness that had built inside his muscles like molten wax.

Then he turned his attention to the spot in which they had stopped and frowned.

The damp sand was going to offer him little comfort, he knew. If, of course, he was capable of sleep.

"Why? Why is—"

Chloe hushed him.

"Let's gather wood and make a fire," She turned her gaze skyward. "It's going to get cold tonight. Might even rain."

"But—"

She turned, and the moonlight lit the scarred crevices in her face like the individual strands of a coarsely braided rope.

"There will be plenty of time to talk, Cal. Now, please, help me gather some wood. Aiden, you stay here and standpoint."

The man had been so silent during their journey that Cal had forgotten he was even with them. When he looked at Aiden, he realized that his form appeared more solid in the moonlight. Not completely opaque—Cal could still make out a sort of low definition representation of the sand behind him if he turned his head at a particular angle—but not as waif-like as before.

Yes, everyone had made a sacrifice in this war for the Marrow.

Chapter 19

"I'M NOT SURPRISED. EVERYONE comes across the Curator at least once in their lives. Most people don't even notice him—or her—they just pass by without knowing. Some though... some are *touched*."

Cal stared into the flames, watching them as they ascended upward, dancing their seductive dance. Just when he thought he saw some sort of image, made sense of their twisting shape, they evaporated into the moonlight.

"I didn't pass him by," he said softly. "Or at least he didn't pass me by. He spoke to me, told me things, things that I didn't—still don't—completely understand."

Silence fell over he and Chloe, and Cal took this moment to look down at his friend as he had done repeatedly over the last few hours.

To see if Robert was still breathing.

And he was. Robert's chest rose slowly and then fell. He was enveloped in a deep, deep sleep, something that Cal envied. Exhaustion had wrapped its long fingers around his chest and had started to squeeze.

"The Curator has been around for a long time, Cal. A long, long time. Even longer than I have, and maybe even Sean Sommers, before his time was up. There are things that he knows, of which I am not even privy. Things about the nature of this world, about the Marrow, about doorways."

Doorways? Doorways to where?

He shook his head, fighting back memories of that day back in Mooreshead. With all that had happened over the past six months or so, he felt his mind might shatter like Robert's if he started to relive that, too.

"What's going to happen here, Chloe? What's Leland's endgame?"

Chloe didn't answer for so long that Cal thought that she might have fallen asleep by the fire like her son.

"Chl—"

She raised her face to look at him, her lipless mouth stretching into a thin, emotionless line.

"Leland has one goal: to open a rift in the Marrow. To allow quiddity to flow from the Marrow and back into this world," she paused before continuing. "Something happened to him, something changed him. He used to be one of us, a guardian. And like me, he worked hard to keep the Marrow a one-way street. Sure, over the decades, there have always been dissidents among our ranks, those who yearned for more. Sometimes these impostors come in the form of religious zealots, other times something just snaps, as happened to Leland, and they go off the rails. They get obsessed with this idea that the self is real, that it's worth preserving, that it's so valuable that it shouldn't simply reside in the Marrow, but it should be here on earth, forever. But it's an illusion, Cal. The self simply doesn't exist."

Cal shook his head. He had heard this rhetoric before, but each successive time he thought he understood it less.

"What does that mean, exactly? I mean, I view the world from my own eyes, view it from my own experience. But *I* don't exist?"

Chloe shrugged.

"You exist, but not in the way that you think you do. There is no little man behind your eyes guiding your actions, no overseer of your being. There is just your biology, which is governed by your experiences and your genetics. And there is also your quiddity, your essence, which brings everything together in a cohesive unit. And this quiddity must be returned to the Marrow so that it can become the glue for others who have yet to be born."

"So, it's... what? Like reincarnation?"

Chloe sighed.

"Yes and no. Not in the religious sense, anyway. People are fascinated by the traditional idea of reincarnation for the most base reasons: you get to live on, *you*, the self which doesn't exist, gets transposed into a new mind, a new body and you get to continue your life journey. This is not quiddity, this is fantasy. There is only life and the Marrow, and the quiddity that must be returned."

Cal let this final sentence sink in for a moment.

"Then what is the Marrow? Why does it exist? What's the point?"

Chloe drew a deep breath, which had a slight whistling sound to it as it passed through where her nose used to be.

"I'm tired, Cal—I need to sleep. And you would be well-advised to do the same. The time when we need to make a stand is nearing, a stand that will be led by Robert, but one that we all have a role to play in. Tomorrow when we meet with the Curator, you will know more. Until then, rest."

Cal debated telling Chloe about the book, the one that he had scribbled furiously in all those years ago—about the tunnels and the tanks that had seemingly come from nowhere, passing through his mind to his arm, his hand, the pencil, and then finally transcribed on the page—but decided against it.

He had secrets, too. And while they might eventually come to the fore, now was not the time.

Chloe was right, they needed to sleep.

But he had just one more question before they packed it in for the night.

"The Marrow... it means the middle, right?"

Chloe nodded, the fire dancing as it reflected off her one good eye.

"But the middle of *what*, exactly?"

Chloe's body had become still.

"Chloe?"

No response.

Cal frowned and shifted his ass in the sand. Then he lay down and stared at the stars high above.

Is this all there is?

***

Water clung to his calves like two puckering, toothless mouths trying to suck the hair from his bare legs.

He looked down then, his eyes drawn to the flickering creatures that passed all around him. At first, he thought they were bioluminescent krill, glowing bright white as they shed their energy. But upon closer inspection, Cal realized that these were no aquatic critters; instead, the glowing objects were reflections of the stars in the night sky above, appearing to dance their pretty dance as energy passed through the water.

Cal felt a sense of serenity, despite being unsure of whether he was dreaming or awake, and if the latter, how he had come to be in the water. It was as if the liquid itself, suckling at his very flesh, was imbued with some sort of drug, a muscle relaxant, that made him feel completely at ease.

He turned his gaze slowly upward, the stars blurring slightly as if smeared with a greasy thumb.

His eyes fell on the brightest star in the sky, a giant, glowing pinprick that started to grow as he stared at it.

It's just my eyes defocussing, he thought, but as he continued to look, he realized that this wasn't the case.

The star really was growing.

Cal squinted, trying to understand what he was seeing.

A supernova? A government satellite? An experiment in deep space?

He had heard of such things, of the government creating cluster bombs in space. Preparing for a war here on earth.

But the stars started to spread out, not in a random pattern as he might expect if it was some sort of explosion. Instead, the stars replicated, duplicated, formed discrete, organized rows.

They almost looked like brushed steel, like tunnels...

Something brushed against Cal's leg, and his eyes, wide now, whipped downward.

This time there *was* an aquatic creature in the water, only it wasn't a miniature crustacean or jellyfish, but a fish... of sorts.

It was thinner and wider than any Cal had seen before, and it had long, flowing tendrils that made up some sort of tail.

For some reason, Cal felt compelled to grab it, and he leaned over to do just that. Only when his hand broke the surface of the water, the fish-like creature flipped onto its side, revealing a scaleless surface roughly the size of a dinner plate.

Cal made out two slits in the side, and then they opened.

Two eyes stared up at him—two large, *human* eyes. And even though they weren't masked by round spectacles, he recognized the pale blue eyes never-the-less.

They were Allan Knox's eyes.

The eyes blinked once, twice, and then Cal started to scream.

Chapter 20

HELEN HUMPHRIES DIDN'T NEED to spring to the surface as she had done twice before. Instead, she simply floated there like foam sitting atop the surface of a swamp.

And yet she didn't kid herself; she knew that Robert was in charge, that he could push her back down at any moment. But she also knew that if she wanted to, Helen could make it difficult for him to do exactly that, and if taken by surprise, well...

It was a strange, exhilarating, *empowering* experience when she was in control of Robert Watts's body. Back when Helen had been alive, control was something that had escaped her the same way calculus seemed out of reach in high school; she knew that an answer existed, that the problem could be solved, but the methodology, the steps needed to get there, simply eluded her.

You ain't nothin' but a sack of meat; tits on an incubator. And your fucking incubator's broke, her husband's voice grated. Then he had laughed, tilting his thick chin to the sky, a throaty chuckle aimed upward like some sort of organic thunder.

You can't even fucking do that right!

The truth was, Helen was ashamed. And even if she thought that her degenerate husband would listen, she wouldn't have been able to tell him the truth, that the reason why she couldn't have children was because her father had beaten her when she was little, had whipped and punched her so many times that she had first missed, then stopped having her period altogether. The doctors said she had a cyst on her left ovary and that was why it was difficult to conceive, but Helen didn't believe them.

She knew the truth.

Her father had beaten her so badly one night that she hadn't been able to take a deep breath, let alone sleep. And these cramps, the worst cramps she had ever experienced, had kept her near or on the toilet for hours.

And there had been blood in the bowl, lots of it.

When she had finally gathered the courage to leave home, the day she turned nineteen years of age, Helen left the weathered two-story colonial with the red brick front and off-white siding, vowing never to return.

And she had held that part of the bargain—not returning home—but her first relationship... well, the man had been a splitting image of her father, complete with the same thinning hair, same scowl, but most damaging was the fact that he had the same temper.

It was her fault, she knew. Not all of it, of course, not in the way that she had done something to deserve the punishment she took first from her father—*You little shit, you think that you can track mud in here and just go about your merry fucking way? Oh, oh, oh, nooo. You are sadly mistaken. You will clean this with your* fucking *tongue*—and then from her husband—*the dishes still ain't clean? Still? And you've been home all day, doing what... exactly?*—but she had had plenty of opportunities to stop it.

The first time Frank Humphries had laid a hand on her had been *his* first time as well. He slapped Helen across the cheek, not in pure fury, but with something akin to trepidation. And then his eyes had changed, and in that moment—in that split-second—Helen could have altered the course of not only her own history, but perhaps the history of a woman after her, or maybe two or three who might happen across Frank Humphries in their time, but she hadn't—Helen had done nothing.

And when no divine or secular power had intervened, Frank's eyes had changed again. They went dark. And they would remain dark until her own vision turned black as his fist collapsed the side of her face.

She had waited so long to respond, to actually do anything to help herself, that when she finally tried, it was too late.

Far too late.

Helen was like the boxer who had already lost the fight, the ref was holding her while at the same time trying to wave his arms and signal that the match was indeed over.

She pawed at Frank as he struck her, which only served to infuriate him further.

How dare she respond this way *now*? After all this time? After the precedent had been set, after the pattern had been established.

And then, Helen Humphries had died.

Only she hadn't, not really, not all the way.

The darkness of death that she had expected had encompassed her, but while her visual senses had been obliterated, *something* remained. There was something in that void.

A voice. One that called to her.

Hellllennnnn, Helllennnn.

A masculine voice, one dripping with authority, one to which she was compelled to listen.

Hellllllennn, I need you to do something for me.

Helen felt her head nod up and down, despite the fact that she no longer had a head or even a body to actually move.

The next thing she heard was the rain. The sound, but not the sensation as even though the water pelted down on her—she heard it, saw it, smelled it, almost tasted it—it didn't seem to touch her.

Confused, Helen turned her head skyward, expecting the careening droplets to force her to blink, but that didn't happen either.

The drops appeared to simply pass *through* her. Helen raised her palms next, confusion washing over her.

It's my eye, she thought, as she tried to grow accustomed to her monocular vision. *It's just strange, something I need to get used to.*

But with her palms up, she realized that she couldn't feel the drops on her skin. And her skin… it had a strange, bluish tinge to it, and if she focused hard enough, Helen could pick up the sight of wet grass *through* her hands.

This made her feel nauseous, and she decided not to consider it for a while, at least.

After all, there were more pressing questions to deal with. Starting with figuring out how she had gone from being pummeled by her husband in her living room to being here, outside in the rain.

Alone.

Confused.

Headlights suddenly lit up the night, and Helen instinctively crouched down and scooted backward. She was at the side of the road, she realized, at the edge of a small, overgrown area that might have at one time been the borders of the woods, but had since been clawed back to make room for more roads, infrastructure, townhouses.

But then she saw something else. A little girl, eight maybe nine years of age, her head down, her pace slow, trodden. She was on the sidewalk, but the car that approached was taking the corner too quickly on the rain-slick road.

Helen realized what was going to happen, and started to move.

And then the voice spoke to her again, and her actions were magnified.

Now! Go to her now!

Helen leaped forward, not thinking of what she was doing. It was a terrible mistake.

The girl would have been better off if Helen had stayed in the woods, maybe even more so if she had remained dead after Frank Humphries had killed her.

Helen saw the woman's face clearly through the windshield, her pretty, heart-shaped features illuminated by the ambient glow of a cell phone.

Their eyes met, and the mouth of the woman behind the wheel parted in a scream. In order to avoid Helen, she yanked the steering wheel to the right and aimed the two-ton hunk of metal and plastic directly at the young girl in the soggy sneakers who continued to walk, head down, wet hair dripping in front of her face.

And then Helen was gone again, surrounded by the velvety blanket of darkness, only to return in a derelict Crematorium some months later, a single thought echoing in her mind: *Amy.*

Chapter 21

AIDEN KINKAID WATCHED CAL rise from his slumber, staring in confusion at the whites of the man's eyes which were visible between thin slits.

What the fuck is he doing?

After Chloe and Cal had fallen asleep, Aiden had receded away from the fire, taking up post against a small outcropping of rocks roughly fifty yards from where they lay.

He didn't need to sleep, at least not anymore. Three times since he had been stabbed to death by Bella behind the Harlop Estate Aiden had tried to get some shut-eye. The first time, he hadn't even closed his eyes before his mind filled to the brim of images of his own death, of his blood leaking out of him, his hair being pulled back, Carson's sour breath on his cheek as he taunted him.

He hadn't slept that night.

Expecting to be exhausted the following day, Aiden had been surprised when he had felt as spry as ever. Still, knowing that it would eventually catch up to him, he tried to sleep the following night, but again he dreamed of death. Only this time, it wasn't *his* death. It was someone else's: a slight woman who shrieked as BBQ sauce-stained knuckles caved her head in.

And thus, sleep had evaded him for a second straight night. And yet, when the sun rose, Aiden didn't feel the icy grip of fatigue, the slow thudding of his heart in his chest, reminiscent of his days in Iraq when he had gone close to 72 hours without resting, then hopped up on a mixture of coffee grains and chewing tobacco. But he just felt... strangely normal.

And yet, despite this revelation, the third night after his death, Aiden Kinkaid had once again attempted to sleep.

This time had been different.

There had been death—there was always death when he closed his eyes, even when he was still alive—but it wasn't a specific person's death that he witnessed. Instead, Aiden experienced an odd brooding sensation, like thunder that originated inside his chest, which was quickly followed by a blast of icy coldness.

Then there was the voice, the one that ordered him to *cooooome* to the Marrow, to give himself up to its liquid shores. It was a disembodied voice, ethereal, seeming without identity, without context, as if it were uttered not only over a long distance, but time as well.

The idea was foreign to him, and he was beginning to think that not all his thoughts were his anymore. That somehow when he had died, he had gained access to something more.

Something bigger.

That voice...

Aiiiiden, you need to coooome. You need to give yourself to the Marrow. Aiiiiideeeeen... Aaiiiiiiiiiiiideennnnnnn... cooooooome.

He had tried to wake then, which shouldn't have been that difficult considering that he wasn't sleeping, not really, but to his horror, he had found that his eyelids were glued together.

Aiiiiiiiiiiiiiidennnnnnnnn.

Like an airy whisper skipping over an impossibly large body of water, his name fluttered to him.

When he finally managed to tear his eyes open, he realized that several hours had passed.

That was the last time Aiden Kinkaid had tried to sleep.

His friends, however...

He watched as Cal moved toward the lapping waves with a staggering, almost robotic gait.

What the hell is he up to?

Something else had changed after the Orphanage, after the demon known as the Goat had managed to haul itself out of its own personal hell and into this world.

Cal glowed brighter now.

Since his death, Aiden found himself able to see people's quiddity exuding from their flesh, and also buried deep inside, like a heat signature reminiscent of the night vision goggles he used to wear in the field. It had helped him back at the Orphanage—helped him easily pick out the dead with their weak signals from having one foot in the Marrow, from the bright lights that were Cal, Robert, Shelly, and his one-time employer Sean.

It was an odd thing to stare at, something that took getting used to, but like his inability to sleep, Aiden adapted.

And ever since Robert had fallen into a deep slumber, Cal's quiddity had started to glow brighter and brighter.

Now, ankle deep in water, Aiden had a difficult time staring directly at his friend. Cal's form, arms outstretched, glowed a brilliant yellow-orange and pixelated color seemed to drift from the tips of his fingers, like dust being blown off a tabletop by a sharp breeze.

He has a larger role to play in this.

The thought materialized in Aiden's mind out of nowhere, as if conjured by the ethos itself.

Or from the Marrow. Maybe it came from the Marrow.

He's more important than he knows... and I need to protect him.

Aiden slipped the rifle off his back and brought the sight to his eye.

As Cal bent and stared into the water, transfixed, Aiden followed his gaze. At first, he saw nothing but the reflection of the man's quiddity which sent brilliant, colorful streaks radiating outward across the calm water.

And then he saw something else.

Aiden blinked hard, trying to make out the details.

Was it… seaweed?

It almost looked like tiny stalks of seaweed breaching the surface of the water around Cal's ankles.

But it couldn't be seaweed, because it appeared to be moving in the opposite direction of the current.

Aiden swallowed hard and nestled the butt of the gun against his right shoulder, squinting into the eyepiece.

It wasn't seaweed, he realized in horror, but fingers.

As he watched, dozens of fingertips first broke the surface, followed by hands. Grabbing, grasping hands all trying to seize Cal's puckered skin and yank him under.

Aiden's finger slipped from the trigger guard to the actual trigger, but Cal's body suddenly straightened and as he did, the hands receded back beneath the waves. And then Cal started back toward shore.

Aiden lowered the rifle.

When Cal made it all the way back to his spot on the beach and lowered his body into the groove in the sand, he moved the gun to his lap.

Aiden sighed, closed his eyes in a slow blink, and as expected, he heard the voice again.

Aiiiiiiiiiiiiiidennnnnnnn… cooooooome…

Only this time it wasn't like before; this time, the sound seemed to have a direction.

Aiden's eyes snapped open and he flicked his head to the right.

He didn't immediately notice anything out of the ordinary, but when he brought the scope back to his face, he made out several figures moving toward them, staying close to the rock face, hugging the shadows.

It was a woman and at least half a dozen children.

Chloe had told them that Leland wouldn't chase them here, that they already had what they needed — that all they wanted was Shelly and her baby.

But someone was coming — someone had sent Bella and the guardian orphans after them.

Aiden got to his feet and walked briskly toward the small fire on the beach that was on the verge of burning out.

They had to get moving again, and fast.

The dead were coming for them.

Chapter 22

"**Did you feel that?**" Allan Knox asked, turning his eyes skyward.

Ed the Nose followed his gaze.

The sky had started to go dark, which was surprising, given the fact that ever since they had arrived in this strange place — the Marrow, if the stories Ed had been told were to be believed — the sky had been bright, balmy, impossibly perfect.

Now, however, he realized that Allan was right: a hint of clouds had started to roll in from the south... or what he thought was the south, anyway. Not *dark* clouds, but the white fluffy kind. Ed wasn't sure what this meant, but he was fairly certain that it wasn't a good omen.

Not here, anyway.

"Yeah, I feel it," Ed answered. And he *did* feel it, he felt a certain pressure in his chest, as if he were coming down with something. Like a cold, maybe.

The thought almost made him laugh out loud.

The dead getting the flu.

He swallowed dryly and the humor passed.

"I feel it, and it ain't good."

They had been walking along the beach for several hours now, looking for anything, anything at all, that might offer them relief from the monotony. There was the island, of course, a dark green swash amidst the calm blue of the sea, but there was no way that Ed was going back into the water again. Not after last time, after he was nearly overcome with the desire to lay back and spread his arms as he fell into it.

He knew what it meant, or at least he thought it did; the Marrow wanted him.

But Allan was right; there was more for them to do. Like the pressure in his chest, the notion that they weren't quite done yet was a tangible sensation.

And the island was the key.

The problem was, of course, that there was no way to get to it.

"Hey, you see that?" Allan asked softly.

Ed lowered his eyes from the island on the horizon and followed the boy's finger.

There, on the beach ahead of them, was something that Ed could only describe as a shimmer, like droplets of oil dancing across a mirror. It was a strange illusion, one that made his stomach flip. He swallowed and looked away, focusing on the sand to clear his head before looking back.

The shimmer was gone, but in its place was a worn, wooden canoe, not fifty paces from where they were presently standing.

Ed blinked twice, confirmed as best he could that it wasn't a mirage, then turned to Allan.

"You, uh, you see that?"

Allan nodded subtly, his chin barely moving. He pulled his thick glasses from his nose, cleaned them quickly on the hem of his shirt, and then put back on.

"A canoe," he confirmed. "But where did it come from?"

Ed glanced around, his eyes drifting from the canoe to the clouds above, to the island in the distance.

Then he remembered something that Robert told him, or maybe it was one of the others, the strange person in the black hood, perhaps, or Cal or Shelly.

The walls are weakening, the divide between our world and the Marrow is becoming thinner.

Is that what's happening here? Ed wondered as his eyes drifted back to the canoe. *Is this object from our world? Was it —*

But Ed didn't finish the thought. As he stared, a hunched man dressed in dark rags not so much stood as unfurled his body, revealing himself from behind the canoe.

Ed, so surprised by the man's appearance, reached for Allan, only to find that the boy was doing the same. They clumsily clutched each other's forearms, and Allan gasped audibly.

The man in rags shook his entire body like a puppy emerging from his first swim, then leveled the palest blue eyes that Ed had ever seen at them.

"I'm thinking that y'all need a ride, am I right?" the man said. Then he grinned, revealing teeth so caked with filth that it looked like he had a mouth full of dirt.

Chapter 23

"THEY'RE GAINING ON US," Chloe rasped. "They'll catch us before nightfall."

Cal grunted as he adjusted his grip on the travois handles. His palms were shredded, and so many blisters had formed and popped that he thought his fingers had pruned.

"I'm going as fast as I can," he grumbled. Cal turned to look down at Robert, who was lying on his back, eyes closed, arms crossed over his chest like a man in a casket.

He really was moving as quickly as possible, except he was compelled to stop every few minutes to make sure that his friend was still breathing, still alive.

"It's not fast enough," Chloe repeated, peering back along the beach that they had come.

"Well, sorry I'm not Ben fucking John—"

Chloe hushed him by raising a finger, and Cal's brow furrowed.

"What? What is it?" he whispered. "What do you see?"

Chloe closed her good eye and remained completely still. The only sound aside from the slow waves lapping at the shore was the whistle that her breathing made as air pushed through her mangled nose.

For a moment, Cal feared that she had fallen into the same deep sleep or coma that Robert had succumbed to, and that he would be alone with their two motionless bodies on this fucked up beach.

And then he would just give up. He would walk into the water and just keep on walking until the cold liquid filled his—

Chloe's eye snapped open and focused on him.

"We need to hurry."

Cal frowned.

"You said that already, and I told you, I'm hurrying, for fuck's sake. That's what—"

A sound, a splash of sorts, drew Cal's attention.

What he saw immediately caused him to drop the travois. Robert, a mere afterthought now, flopped to one side and nearly slid off the side.

"Oh my God," Cal whispered.

Three heads broke the surface of the water—three small, round heads, hair and grime clinging to their scalps in thin clumps. Two of the three were young girls judging by their long, dark hair, but the rest of their features were nearly indistinguishable irrespective of gender.

Horribly indistinguishable.

What was left of the flesh covering their skulls was sallow, hanging from their cheeks and chins in tendrils like congealed milk. Where their eyes used to be there were only gaping holes, deep, dark caverns reminiscent of the dead eyes of the animated corpses from the crematorium.

The reason for this soon became obvious: these three kids, children, no more than seven, maybe eight years of age, were also dead.

Long dead.

Cal felt his heart fall into his stomach, making friends with the perpetual knot nestled within.

These were three of the children from the orphanage.

And they were coming for them.

Cal turned to Chloe, who was staring at the corpses with a sort of strange reverence.

Do something! Fucking do something! Cal's mind screamed, but despite his mental command, he too felt unable to move.

The children started to move forward, walking as if on land, unencumbered by the water that hugged first their chins, then their necks, and before Cal could fully comprehend what was going on, their shoulders.

Cal glanced down at Robert for support next, but his friend simply lay on one side of the travois, motionless.

Wake the fuck up, Robert! We need you, now! Wakey-wakey, eggs and fucking rotten bakey!

But Robert didn't wake up.

He didn't do anything.

"Chloe—" Cal finally managed to gasp. The word felt thick on his tongue, as if he had been stung by a bee, but before he could add anything else a sonic *thhhwap*, tore by his ear, causing an uncomfortable pressure change that momentarily set him off balance.

The head of the only boy in the group not so much exploded as it vaporized. Bits of gray flesh and bone and whatever else filled the rotting head sprayed backward in a mist that rippled the water like pebbles tossed into a pond. For one, horrifying second, the headless body kept moving, kept walking, keeping stride with the other two guardian children, before slowly collapsing forward.

And then a scream, more of a growl, really, a deep rumbling growl, filled the air.

Chapter 24

AIDEN PUMPED THE SPENT shell from the chamber and was in the process of taking aim again when he heard someone scream.

His first shot had been a direct hit, obliterating the head of the child as he shambled toward Chloe and Cal. So when he heard the shout, his first thought was that it had been one of the other dead, but when he scanned the mouths of the two who remained standing, he saw only teeth pressed together to form lipless grins.

They hadn't screamed; he didn't think that they had the faculties, the anatomy to create such a sound.

Aiden pushed the thoughts from his mind and set about focusing on his next shot, all the while keeping his periphery clear in case Bella made an appearance.

He had watched as the children had first waded out into the water, much like Cal had done hours before, but when they didn't turn back, when they just kept on going, he chalked them up as good as gone, wherever lost quiddity go — *to the Marrow, all quiddity goes to the Marrow. Don't you feel it, Aiden? Don't you feel it? Tugging at you? At your very essence?* — but in the process, he had lost sight of Bella.

But now he had to focus, he had to take out the two other guardian children before they got to Cal and Chloe.

Aiden lined the reticle up with the head of the second child, one with thin, black hair and a gaping wound in one gray cheek. His finger tensed on the trigger, but before he could squeeze off the shot, something suddenly jumped into his field of view.

Aiden pulled the scope away from his eye.

"Don't shoot!" A shout filtered up to him from the beach, "Aiden, don't shoot!"

What the fuck is this?

Chloe had stepped directly between him and the target, her quiddity flaring brightly before his eyes.

What the hell is she doing?

The woman waved her arms above her head, signaling to him as if he were miles away instead of just a couple hundred meters.

"Don't shoot!" she shouted again in her raspy voice.

Cal started to move then, stepping toward Chloe, all the while yelling at her to get out of the way.

The children paid none of this any heed.

They just kept coming.

For a second, Aiden considered firing a round anyway. He squeezed the rifle barrel tightly between his fingers as he contemplated this option. It felt heavier in his hand than it had back on his perch outside the orphanage, something that set off alarm bells in the back of his head.

At the orphanage, his aim had been true, and he had struck down every dead corpse that he had taken aim at. But he had taken a single extra shot. He had fired a single shot at Bella and the bullet had passed right through her; she didn't even seem to notice.

But now was different.

Chloe was different.

And so was he. Ever since Sean Sommers's mummified body had been torn to shreds and the demon that was Leland Black emerged, Aiden felt *different*. More whole, maybe.

And the persistent tug from the Marrow, the one that teased at the back of his mind like an ever-present nagging, asking him to make a choice, to give himself to the Marrow, that had faded a little.

It was still there, but it was no longer as powerful as it had been.

The walls between our world and the Marrow are thinning...

Aiden eased off the trigger and slung the rifle over his shoulder.

Then he hurried down the embankment toward his friends.

Chapter 25

THE SECOND TIME HELEN had emerged from the darkness, she awoke in the crematorium.

The nightmare of her husband beating her to death, now interspersed with images of the little girl in the rain, headlights bearing down, had run on a loop in her mind during the intervening time, which she could only describe as an eternity.

And there was something else, too, a *hint* of something, like sunlight eking around the corner of heavily tinted sunglasses. There was something *good* mixed in with the bad and awful, something that was asking her—

But before Helen could truly grasp what that was, she was pulled back.

I need you again, sweet Helen. I need your help.

And Helen had helped. She helped gather the other dead, helped make sure that the two meddling cops couldn't take Carson and Bella away from *him*.

Before she knew what was happening, Helen found herself at some sort of estate, once again doing the bidding of the voice in her head.

Then she was weeping—as much as a woman missing most of her face and the contents of her skull could weep—as she sent the boy, the skinny boy with the thick glasses, to the Marrow long before his time.

Then Robert had saved her, saved her by condemning her to being locked inside his head, unable to ever get a true sense of the light around the glasses, of the feeling of warmth that she never knew she longed for.

Before Robert had taken her quiddity inside him, completely taken her away from the empty shell of her body, however, the voice had told Helen one final thing.

Something that she tucked away, something that she couldn't even let Robert know.

I will need you once more, Helen. One more time I will call on you before this is over.

And as much as it pained her to be beholden to another man after what had happened, Helen knew, without doubt, that when the voice came calling she would obey.

She had no choice.

Chapter 26

CAL TOOK TWO SMALL steps backward and then tripped over the handle of the travois. With a grunt, he fell in a heap on the sandy beach.

"What are you doing?" he gasped, his eyes locked on the two remaining guardian children who now had almost fully emerged from the water. "Tell Aiden to take them out!"

Chloe shook her head.

"I can't. They're... they're just children, Cal. *My* children. I can't let him just shoot them here on the beach."

Cal stared at the rotting flesh hanging off their round faces, their pitch-black eyes, their arms dangling limply at their sides.

"You've got some ugly ass children," he grumbled under his breath.

"These children," Chloe continued, ignoring his comment. "They were once supposed to protect us from people like my husband," her voice hitched and she lowered her gaze for a moment, "and my son. People like Michael and Bella and Jonah Silvers. They deserve better than this—none of it was their fault. None of *this* is their doing."

Then Chloe Black did the unbelievable. She took a step backward toward the lapping waves behind her.

Cal's eyes, already bulging out of his head, almost exploded when he saw six other orphan children rise from the water behind the first wave.

"Umm, Chloe? You're gonna wanna get over here. Children or not, they're fucking dead and if—"

Once again, Cal's commentary went ignored.

"For decades, I holed myself up in the tower, in *Trellis*, trying to keep things together. And after Carson was incarcerated, I thought that was the end of it. But that bastard... that bastard

Seth had to go and get Robert involved. And now this," she took another step backward. The rotting guardian children were within ten feet of her now, and Chloe didn't seem to care.

"Nice story, Chloe, but maybe you could just—"

"I'm just so tired… after all this time… I'm just so damn tired. I guess I was just too naive to realize it until now, but my time is up, Cal. I'm too old for this fight, too old and too scarred. Too broken. I'm just bringing you down. All this time, I was searching for someone to succeed me without even knowing it, and now I have."

No, please! You can't do this! We need you! Cal's mind shouted as he finally realized what Chloe intended to do.

He turned his gaze to Robert, whose eyes moved frantically from behind closed lids as if he were experiencing the most vivid of dreams.

Wake the fuck up, Robert! Please, you have to stop this insanity.

Chloe took another step backward, and then movement in his periphery forced Cal to whip his head around. He scooted protectively toward Robert, expecting to see another rotting child coming at him from behind this time, trapping them. But it wasn't one of the orphans; instead, it was Aiden, and he too looked frightened.

And it went without saying that something that scared a dead man put the fear of God in Callum Godfrey.

"Chloe, come to me," Aiden snapped, stepping forward.

Chloe shook her head.

"Don't you see? I waited for years for someone to take over, and now that Seth brought Robert into the fold, I've found that person."

Cal swallowed hard and his eyes again moved to Robert at his side, hoping that his friend would suddenly wake up, that

Robert would just *wake the fuck up* and talk some sense into his mother.

Do that weird thing with his hands, maybe, like he had back at the Harlop Estate, and get them out of this mess.

All of them, unscathed.

"Robert can't help us now," Cal whispered, raising his eyes to Chloe's scarred face. "Maybe he can't help us ever again."

"You need to come to me," Aiden said, lowering the gun off his shoulder.

Chloe held up a finger.

"This is it, Aiden," she took another step backward, closing the distance between her and the first of the children to only a handful of feet. "I'm tired, spent. Look at me."

Contrary to the command, Cal looked away from the woman's mangled features, turned his gaze skyward, but when Chloe growled and repeated the words, he leveled his eyes at her.

"Look at me!"

She was bald, the paper-thin layer of skin covering her skull a patchwork of scars from where Leland had cut her all those years ago.

One of her eyes was missing, and her lips were almost completely gone. Her voice, a strangled, hoarse rasp was a consequence of the gash that ran across her throat.

Cal shook his head, trying to prevent his mind from conjuring thoughts of how Chloe must have felt lying on the dusty ground of the abandoned orphanage with her husband's leer reflecting off the knife as he dragged it across the soft skin beneath her chin.

"I didn't know—"

Now it was Cal's turn to interrupt.

"Robert can't help us! You need to come over here, *now*! Get away from them!" Cal screamed as he pulled himself to his feet.

"No, Cal, you don't understand."

She moved backward again, and Cal felt his chest start to quake. Tiny, fleshless fingers at the end of miniature palms suddenly rose and reached for her.

Decades ago, Chloe Black had taught the students, taught them about the Marrow, about what happens after you die and what it meant to keep the Marrow a one-way street.

And she *meant* something to them. Maybe not in their current ragged, decaying forms, but deep down in the quiddity that Cal knew they still possessed, Chloe Black meant something to them.

Cal started to sob.

"Robert can't—"

Chloe shook her head one final time.

"You still don't get it, do you, Cal? I didn't know it myself, not for sure, not until you told me you had met the Curator before and remembered him. Then I knew."

"Chloe, please, you need to—" Aiden began, but the woman had reached the point of no return.

"I don't want Robert to lead the new guardians, Cal," she said with a sigh. "I want you to do it."

The words so stunned Cal that when Chloe abruptly backpedaled, neither he nor Aiden reacted in time.

"No!" Aiden shouted, and he lunged toward the woman, only to pull back again as the children grabbed Chloe's falling body.

Cal stared through teary eyes as their tiny hands started to tug at her cloak all the while dragging her backward into the water.

As their forms started to shimmer—either a consequence of the sun reflecting off the waves, or of their bodies passing over—Cal saw Chloe's ragged slit of a mouth start to open again.

Only this time, he wasn't sure if he heard the words she said, or simply read her lips.

Find the Curator, Cal. Find the Curator and put an end to this before it's too late, before the gates to Hell are open forever.

Chapter 27

ED'S EYES SHOT UPWARD as the cloudy sky suddenly brightened. There was a brilliant flash, one that sent streaks of red and white across his vision, but it only lasted a second. In its wake were more clouds, only these weren't the white and fluffy kind as before. These were ominous, with hints of dark gray licking their edges.

There was a storm brewing, of that he was certain.

"What was that?" he asked absently, only half expecting an answer.

"Another one bites the dust," the man in the rags said with a laugh.

Ed stared at him, a grimace plastered on his face.

"What'd you say?"

The man, who had yet to offer them a name, smiled, revealing his caked brown teeth.

"You don't need to be worrying about that," he replied, grabbing the bow of the boat with two hands and giving it a push toward the water.

Ed looked over at Allan, who simply shrugged as he stared back.

"Who are you?" Ed asked, his police instincts taking over. Even though this was as far from his district—as far from NYC—as humanly possible, he couldn't shut off his detective mind. "Where did you come from?"

The man's hands, covered in what appeared to be tattered wool gloves, squeezed the wooden bow until his fingertips turned white. He stopped pushing and his smile flickered.

"I'm not from here, I'll tell you that much. And I won't be staying long."

Ed didn't like the evasive answer; he had spent too much time among thieves and liars and degenerates to know the reason behind these types of responses. But before he could address this, Allan spoke up.

"You mean you're not coming with us?"

The brown smile returned.

"Heeeelll no," he tittered, "I don't belong here."

Ed's grimace deepened.

"What do you mean you—"

"Whelp, would you look at that," the man in rags said, looking down at a wrist that didn't sport a watch. "My time here is up."

He gave a final shove and the ass end of the boat—a glorified canoe, really—started to sway in the water. Then he waved his hand across it as if showcasing an expensive piece of jewelry.

"So how about you guys get in? You've got somewhere to be as well, don't you, now?"

Chapter 28

AIDEN REACHED FOR CAL'S arm, but he pulled away at the last second.

"Don't touch me," he whispered as he wiped the tears from his eyes with the back of one hand. "Don't fucking touch me."

"We have to go," Aiden said quietly. "We have to—"

"Neat trick you got there," a female voice said from behind them. Cal whipped around and then staggered.

Bella was standing in the sand, feet spread shoulder width apart, hands at her sides.

Aiden stepped around Cal, giving him a protective berth as he placed himself between them.

"Go," he whispered over his shoulder. "Take Robert and run."

Cal stared at the demented woman with the hair that looked as if it had been cut by a child using a meat cleaver.

"Oh, the big bad protector, huh?" Bella twisted her wrist and a blade suddenly appeared in her hand. "We've played this game before, Aiden. And you lost."

Bella flicked her other wrist, and now both hands held six-inch long blades. She strode forward, and Aiden did the same, slipping the gun from his shoulder as he did.

"You tried that, too," she said, and although her face remained stern, Bella seemed to hesitate. "Didn't work."

Cal reached down and grabbed the handles of the travois and then slowly rose again.

Bella smirked as she peeked around Aiden at Cal, and then at Robert.

"Huh, the Black boy not doing so well, is he? Never was the strong one of the two. I'm glad I picked Carson. I mean, he's not perfect, but—"

Cal clenched his teeth.

"What do you want from us?" he suddenly shouted, gripping the handle of the travois as tightly as his blistered hands could manage. "What the fuck do you want from us? You stole Shelly, you have the baby! What more do you want?"

Aiden tried to hush him by holding up a hand, but Cal was suddenly overcome by fury.

"You took everything!" he threw his arms out to his sides. "We're done! Wasted! Spent! Why don't you just leave us the fuck alone?"

Bella fully turned to face him now, flashing the blades in quick, almost hypnotic movements.

"Everything? Oh no, little Black, there's one thing that—"

A shot suddenly rang out, one that took both of them by surprise.

Bella's left shoulder jerked backward, and her face, previously twisted into a lecherous grin, became contorted in pain.

What the fuck?

Cal turned to Aiden and saw that the end of the rifle appeared to be smoking.He stared in disbelief.

"How—" he started, but Aiden interrupted him before he could finish the sentence.

"Go, Cal. Go now. Take Robert and find the Curator."

Cal just gaped.

"Go!"

The shout spurred him to action, and he swiveled on his heels, dragging the travois with Robert's still slumped body behind him. And then he ran.

Cal ran as fast and as hard as his wasted body could manage, all the while Bella's voice trailed after him.

"I'm coming for you, Cal. You *and* Robert. And I won't stop until I kill you all."

Chapter 29

AIDEN CIRCLED TO HIS left, leveling the gun at Bella's chest this time. It was a long-range rifle, and it wasn't designed for this application. Still, it would put a mighty big hole in the woman's chest.

If it hit its mark, that is.

He was still confused as to why the bullet that had struck her in the shoulder had actually done damage. Not as much as it should have—he could only see a spot of blood from the point of impact and she seemed none the worse for wear—but it *had* hurt her.

Unlike back at the orphanage.

Bella shifted to her right, raising her hands with the two blades up in front of her as she did, her injured shoulder a fraction of a second slower than the other. But when she twirled the blades around quickly, so fast that they became blurs of glinting metal, there was no perceptible difference between the two arms.

"I've killed you before, Aiden, and I'm going to do it again. And then I'm—"

Aiden pulled the trigger and the rifle went off a second time, the sound impossibly loud as it reverberated off the rock face behind Bella, and then slid over the surface of the water to his rear.

The water that Chloe had been dragged under, the water that had frothed and boiled as the children took her to the Marrow.

The bullet missed and a moment later a shower of rock shards erupted in the distance.

And then it was Bella's turn. She shifted her weight to one foot, then slid the other way, moving so quickly that Aiden only had time to lean to one side before the blade sliced the skin covering his ribcage.

It was only a shallow wound, but it stung.

It had been a long time since Aiden had *felt* anything and it gave him pause. Bella took advantage of this and slipped behind him, using the blade in her other hand to cut the back of his arm.

Aiden grunted and spun away, while at the same time raising the gun.

He was fast, but like before, Bella was faster. He squeezed off another round, the final in the chamber, but this time it just skipped harmlessly across the water.

The next strike from Bella's blade was no flesh wound.

The entire six-inches of glinting steel slid between Aiden's lower two ribs. He felt a hiss and then something akin to a balloon deflating as his lung was punctured.

Bella was right. She had beaten him before — had *killed* him before — and she had done so with blades not unlike these. And this offered Aiden an unusual advantage. Instead of falling away from the strike, as he might have done previously, Aiden twisted, and as he predicted, the knife remained lodged between his ribs, while Bella's grip failed.

Bella laughed and sprang back, and Aiden tossed the now useless gun to the ground. His side hissing, and his breathing sounding much the same, Aiden brought his hands out in front of him like some sort of bear rising up against a much smaller prey.

I don't need the gun... all I need is to get my hands on her. All I need to do is grab her and we'll both go to the Marrow. And this can all be over.

Bella seemed to read his mind.

"You're too slow, old man. Carson told me about you... said he saw things, saw things in his visions. *Baaaaad* things that you done."

Aiden tried to ignore her, but her words took him by surprise.

"And you know what? I realized something. We know someone in common, Aiden Kinkaid ex-militia—"

Aiden lunged, trying to catch Bella by surprise. And he did. Bella's eyes widened, and she reared away from him.

He would have grabbed her, would have wrapped his hands around her throat and strangled her right then and there, sending them both to the Marrow, if Bella hadn't tripped.

The usually sure-footed killer's heel struck a piece of half-burnt wood from the fire and she fell on her backside, sending a small puff of soot into the air.

Aiden's lunge was so complete that he found himself airborne, the knife still lodged in his side thankfully keeping his lung from deflating.

He overshot his mark and as soon as Bella hit the ground, she rolled out of the way.

All Aiden got was a face full of dirt.

He grunted as a second blade slid into him just above his right hip. This time, it retracted before Aiden could twist it out of Bella's hand.

The pain was intense, a blinding heat that sent his entire left side alight.

The next strike sheared his upper thigh, and the one after that—the two strikes happening in such rapid succession that Aiden thought Bella might have gotten her first blade back—sliced his upper arm.

Aiden cried out, then rolled to one side. As he did, he scooped up a handful of soot from the fire and flung it.

For once, luck was on his side.

The gray cloud hit Bella in the face and she immediately stopped stabbing him, and instead tried to wipe it from her eyes.

Aiden rose like a prehistoric beast, a wounded animal, and staggered after her.

"No!" Bella shrieked. "No!"

Blinded, Bella continued to rub at her eyes, all the while moving backward toward the water.

This is my chance, Aiden thought, *all I have to do is touch her.*

It was as if time itself dilated as he tried repeatedly, and failed, to grab the woman.

Aiden wouldn't have noticed that he was ankle deep in water now if Bella hadn't reached down and scooped some of the cool liquid with the hand not holding the knife and splashed her face.

Her gray mask became black streaks.

Aiden's breathing had become labored, and he didn't dare look down at his side to see if he had dislodged the knife when his clumsy lunge had missed.

Either way, his liver was sliced, his leg was mangled, and his right arm had been effectively rendered useless.

It was now, or it was forever.

Aiden made a final lunge, but he was in far worse shape than he had predicted and he missed by a wide margin. He collapsed to one knee, the water reaching to mid-thigh.

But then Bella made a mistake.

It might have been her only one, but one mistake was all a man with Aiden's training needed.

He might be old, he might be slow, but he had experience.

When Bella swung what was to be the death blow, aiming for the side of his neck, Aiden didn't pull away. That was what someone with *Bella's* experience expected, which would have made her aim even more accurate.

Instead, Aiden shifted *into* the arc of the strike.

The blade didn't puncture his throat as intended, but overshot the mark and instead slid into the back of his neck where it grated against his vertebrae.

Bella cried out and let go of the knife, but it was too late.

Aiden grabbed her arm, tucking it deep into his armpit.

It's over now... I'm going to the Marrow and I'm taking you with me...

For a moment, nothing at all seemed to happen. Bella seemed frozen, and Aiden couldn't have moved even if he wanted to.

Then the sky started to open and a beautiful warmth inundated both of them.

Still clenching his armpit, Aiden turned his face upward, reveling the feeling of warmth—such beautiful, calming, *amazing* warmth—as it passed through him, and then he closed his eyes.

Time passed—how much, however, Aiden had no idea.

But then Bella started to try to wrench her arm free. Aiden's eyes snapped open, and he realized that the sky had closed up again.

A deep, shuddering sigh passed through him then, and he looked down at Bella's face.

"Alright," he said more to himself than to Bella, "we'll do this the old-fashioned way."

Aiden loosened his grip on Bella's arm the second he felt her trying to pull again. Not expecting this, her thin body flung backward, and she landed on her back in the water.

Aiden pounced again, this time landing directly on top of her.

He reached into the water, knocking away her thrashing and flailing arms until his fingers found Bella's throat.

And then he started to squeeze.

Through the shimmering surface, Bella looked up at him while her hands desperately tried to claw his fingers away. But without her knifes, without being able to use her speed, she was no match for Aiden.

He squeezed and squeezed, watching as her eyes grew wider while at the same time her thrashing started to lose its fervor.

"Die you fucking bitch!" he screamed as he strangled the woman.

We have a common acquaintance... you've been a baaaad boy, Aiden Kinkaid.

To his surprise, Aiden realized that there were tears streaming down his cheeks.

A bubble suddenly formed in Bella's mouth, which quickly rose to the surface where it broke and disappeared.

She can't know about that... no one knows about that.

There was a second bubble, and then a third.

Then the thrashing stopped altogether.

Aiden held Bella underwater for a full minute after she stopped moving before he let her go. Once released, her body remained suspended a foot below the surface.

Then he staggered toward the shore. His vision had started to blur, and he became acutely aware that he was listing terribly to one side.

Still, he made it to the beach.

Barely.

Once there, he collapsed on his back and stared up at the sky.

"Will you open for me?" he whispered.

When there was no response, he reached into his vest pocket with his left hand — the right was no longer functional — and pulled out a tin of chewing tobacco. After several attempts, he managed to flick the top off with one hand. The inside was still relatively dry, and he pinched as much as he could between thumb and forefinger, letting the rest of the tin fall to the ground.

With a sigh, he tucked the fine strands into the space between his teeth and bottom lip.

Then he shut his eyes and reached across his body to pull out the blade buried in the back of his neck.

A pressure released in his head, and his vision started to swirl.

Aiden spat tobacco juice on the front of his shirt, then opened his eyes again, staring up at the sky, hoping, willing it to open again.

To beam the warmth down on him.

"Will you take me now?" he whispered as darkness washed over him. "Will you take me now?"

Chapter 30

SHELLY WAS FEVERISH, DRIFTING in and out of consciousness in alternating hot and cold flashes.

She saw streaks of light, felt hurricane winds tearing her apart, experienced a crushing sensation in her chest, in her belly.

Twice she had smelled the brine of the Marrow, and both times she had thought that she was on her way.

Her mind was so muddled that she thought of nothing but acceptance.

My time to go.

But both times, someone had splashed cold water on her face, bringing her back from the depths. Shelly thought she remembered someone pouring liquid into her mouth, and maybe a pill or two, but couldn't be certain.

After what she had seen, what she had been through, she had a hard time separating what was real, what was a memory, and what was pure unadulterated fantasy.

Her mind flashed from her time at the orphanage as a young child, then to when Sean had dropped her off at the church.

And then there was Robert—more specifically, her and Robert, and their child—living at his grandfather's house, playing in the backyard while he sipped beer, huffed on a cigar and watched TV.

That couldn't be real… could it?

A pain in her abdomen shocked her back to the present, what she had grown to accept as her new reality.

She groaned, and tried to massage her stomach, to cradle her now huge belly—*how is it possible that it has grown so quickly*—but something hard bit into her wrists and she winced.

Shelly opened her eyes and blinked rapidly, trying to catch her bearings.

"Where am I?" she asked in a hoarse whisper.

There was no answer.

She was in some sort of white-washed room, with cracked subway tiles lining the walls.

"Where—" she started again, but when she tried to turn her head, she found that there were bindings on her throat as well.

Panic started to build in her and she made fists, and then ground her wrists against the bindings.

"Robert? Cal?" she shouted.

The only reply was her own echo.

Shelly tried her legs next, but they too were bound.

"Anyone? *Help me!*"

A sudden intense pain in her abdomen caused her to shriek in pain. Tears started streaming down her cheeks now, and she felt a pressure between her legs.

Shelly stared at her stomach, watching in horror as a shadow passed beneath her skin, which was suddenly mottled and covered in spider webs of blue veins that hadn't been there moments before.

The pressure continued to build, now enveloping her lower abdomen and between her legs.

And then Shelly saw it just beneath the surface of her skin: a narrow, pointed outline of a shape she had seen before.

She recognized it as one of the talons that had been burnt into Robert's calf.

The pain suddenly reached a crescendo, and Shelly screamed.

Mercifully, it only lasted a moment before there was a pop, and then wetness soaked her lower half.

She groaned and tried to tuck her chin in and look at herself, but her bindings prevented her from seeing anything below her massive belly.

"Oh god," she moaned, "oh god, oh god, what's happening to me?"

Something's not right... it's too... sticky... something's not right... something's not right...

She threw her head back and closed her eyes, breathing quickly through pursed lips.

It's too soon, her mind screamed. *It's too soon! The baby can't be coming now!*

Her lower legs went numb, and she felt her groin contract so tightly that she thought if her hands and feet weren't bound, she would have curled into a ball the size of a peanut.

It was too soon, but that didn't change the fact that the baby was coming.

As if to reinforce her thoughts, a voice sounded somewhere to her left. A deep, rumbling voice that seemed to come from everywhere and nowhere at the same time.

"The baby's coming soon—we need to get ready."

PART III – TASTE OF THE

MARROW

Chapter 31

"Mr. Underhill, can you hear me? Mr. Underhill?"

Dr. Simon Transky, affectionately referred to as *Si* by his colleagues in equal parts due to this Jewish heritage as to his love of the active ingredient in magic mushrooms, *psilocybin*, snapped his fingers in front of the bearded man's face.

"Mr. Underhill?"

The sound of a creaking chair made Si turn from the patient to face the other doctor in the room. Dr. Muller was older than Si by about a decade, maybe more, and with that came experience. And with experience came a level of smugness known only to physicians. The man crossed his arms atop his considerable belly and smirked.

"I told you he won't answer," Dr. Muller said without so much as looking at Si.

Si shrugged and snapped his fingers again.

This time, Mr. Landon Underhill blinked and he seemed, at least for a fleeting moment, to snap out of his stupor.

"Wendy? Is that you, Wendy?"

Si raised an eyebrow and leaned in close, putting his elbows on his knees.

"No, it's not Wendy. My name is Dr. Transky, but you can call me Si. Listen, Mr. Underhill, do you —"

"Robert? Is that you, Robert?"

Si's eyes narrowed.

"No," he said slowly. He reached out and touched the man's leg, and Landon turned his head to face him. His eyes were dark and cloudy now.

"Cal? Shelly? Aiden? Sean? Helen?"

Si leaned away again, taken aback by the flatness of the man's voice as much as the strangeness of the words themselves.

He turned to face Dr. Muller.

"Is this…"

Muller nodded.

"Yep, always the same: *Robert, Cal, Shelly, Helen, Aiden, Sean.* Sometimes Wendy, although not as often these days."

"And I assume you tried to track these people down? Find out if they're real?"

"…*Shelly, Robert, Helen…*"

"Oh, we tried. Had some success, too. When he first came in here with severe PTSD and schizoid tendencies, we were able to piece together the last few months before his life went off the rails. Best we figure it, this guy was fucking —"

Si's eyes bulged and he tilted his head quickly at Landon, reminding Muller that the patient was sitting right there in the room with them.

Dr. Muller waved a hand dismissively.

"Oh, it doesn't matter. He doesn't respond to anything. Here, watch this," Muller turned to Landon and snapped his fingers. "Your mother is a fucking whore."

Si swallowed hard and waited for Landon's reaction.

"Shelly? Cal? Robert? Is that you?"

Dr. Muller leaned back and shrugged.

"See what I mean? He's locked in traction. Anyways, as I was saying, best we could work out from friends and colleagues was that Landon was fucking the wife of one of his employees, but she died in a car accident while leaving his house. Her kid died, too. Sad shit, really. The wife's name was Wendy and the husband was Robert. As for the others? Your guess is as good as mine. Robert's long gone, and he seemed to have taken Landon's soul with it."

Si frowned as he observed the patient. Landon was pale, thin, with a thick, dark beard that covered his face and neck. He tried not to feel pity for the man—*don't feel pity for him, he's not your friend, he's your patient*—but he couldn't quite help it.

Landon just looked so damn... sad.

"When he first came in," Dr. Muller continued, "he was talking about voices in his head, about not even wanting to sleep with Wendy. Best guess? Guilt became this sort of weird fantasy in his mind. Over the past few weeks, things have gotten worse. Only says those names, over and over, occasionally sprinkling in a terribly annoying 'is that you?'"

Si took this all in stride.

"... *Robert... Shelly... Cal...*"

"Anyways, that's the story here, your lesson for the day. Extreme PTSD with schizoid tendencies and traction."

Dr. Muller stood, and Si did the same.

"Thank you, Dr. Muller. Thank you for showing me this, the FBI is grateful for your support."

Dr. Muller nodded and they shook hands.

Si turned and was heading toward the door when a thought occurred to him and he looked back.

"Dr. Muller?"

"Yeah?"

"What was the girl's name?"

Dr. Muller's mouth twisted and he scratched the top of his head.

"The girl who died? I think... uh... I think it was —"

Landon Underhill's head suddenly snapped up and his eyes, clear now, as clear a set of pupils that Si had ever seen, trained on him.

"Her name's Amy and she's trapped on an island," he whispered.

Dr. Muller gasped.

Chapter 32

CAL DIDN'T LOOK BACK, not once.

He heard the shots, heard the screams, the shouts of pain and frustration. Sobbing, he lowered his head, tightened his grip on the handles of the travois, and ran.

He ran until the beach thinned, until the sand was slowly replaced by some sort of broadleaf vegetation, and until the water itself had receded out of sight.

Eventually, Cal stopped running. Or, more accurately, his entire body simply shut down. It wasn't a slow process, like a person's movements during exposure to extreme cold. Instead, it was like a car running out of gas.

Cal sputtered, staggered, then simply fell on his face. He barely had the strength to break his fall.

He had no idea how long he had been running, or if he had put enough distance between himself and the orphanage, Bella, Carson, and the Goat.

But he simply couldn't move any longer — his body failed to respond to any of his mental commands.

As his lids started to flutter, he heard something on the wind, a buzzing that grew louder and louder like a bee slowly circling his ear before deciding that it was as good a place as any to nestle in and pollinate.

***

Thwup twhup thwup

Cal opened his eyes and saw sky all around him: it was above him, it was below, it was on either side. Air rushed by his face and ears, sending his hair swirling about his head.

Thwup thwup thwup

***

Thwup twhup thwup

The sky was still all around him, but it was darker now, as night had eclipsed the day.

Cal still heard the buzzing, whirring sound, but now he heard something else as well.

A voice, one that he didn't recognize. The words struggled to complete with the roaring air, but Cal could make out enough to know that it wasn't Carson or the devil himself speaking.

"T-minus one-hour-twenty until touchdown in Mooreshead," the voice exclaimed.

What? Mooreshead? What are—

Cal tried to push himself to his feet, but groaned and collapsed back onto his face.

Thwup twhup thwup

***

Thwup twhup thwup

A face, a round face, young and pretty, blond hair spilling from behind ears that were slightly too large, rose to greet him.

Cal smiled and tried to reach for her, to caress her soft cheek, but his ravaged fingers fell short.

"Stacey? That you? I've missed you so much... so, so much..."

There was a pause, and Cal felt his neck sag.

"He's going out again," a voice said, and although it was an announcement rather than a command, Cal felt himself obeying none-the-less.

Thwup twhup thwup

***

Thwup twhup thwup

This time when Cal opened his eyes, the face he saw wasn't of a young woman, but of a man in his late fifties, his mouth a thin line surrounded by a network of wrinkles.

Wrinkles that screamed authority and experience without saying anything at all.

"Cal?" the man asked. His voice, like his face, was unapologetic.

Cal groaned and somehow managed to shift himself into a seated position.

"Why couldn't it be Stacey?" he grumbled. He used his palms to push his back against something hard, supportive, and in the process, came to the terrible realization that he couldn't feel his hands at all.

He raised them and stared in horror at the mangled trails of flesh, the rawness from popped blisters so complete that it was as if his skin had melted.

And this, in turn, reminded him of the rotting children walking out of the water, their hands outstretched, reaching for Chloe.

His breath caught in his throat and he whipped his face around.

"Who are you?" he snapped, trying to scoot backward, forgetting that he was butted up against something hard. "Who the fuck are you?"

The man reached for him then, and Cal swatted his hand away.

"Don't fucking touch me! Tell me who you are!" his eyes darted. "And where's Robert?"

The man's lips tensed.

"Cal, you're okay... please, you need to calm down."

With more effort than he thought he had in him, Cal managed to stand only to bang his head on the low roof, forcing him to stoop. His thighs and calves screamed in protest, but he did his best to ignore them.

There were more important matters to attend to than some muscle pain.

"Robert! Where's Robert?" he demanded. He tried rubbing the back of his head, but the inability to feel his own body was so strange that he stopped immediately.

The man moved backward and held his palms up, the universal gesture for *'I mean no harm'*.

"You need to calm down, Cal. You're in a helicopter and we've just landed."

T-minus one-hour-twenty to Mooreshead...

Cal shook his head.

"That's not what I asked—I want to know where Robert is."

The man hooked a thumb over his shoulder and Cal followed the gesture with his eyes. Robert was still lying on the travois, but now he was on the grass and another man was hovering over him.

"Get away from him!" Cal snapped. He ducked his head and leaped out of the helicopter. His landing was awkward and his weak leg muscles nearly buckled. Somehow, however, he managed to remain on his feet. "Get the fuck away from him!"

"He's a doctor, Cal," the man from the helicopter said as he hurried to keep up. "Robert... he's in some sort of coma."

"No shit," Cal spat as he continued toward the man. "Get away!"

The man, a doctor, if what stern-face said was to be believed, leaned away from Robert and stood.

He *looked* like a doctor, if there was such a thing, but Aiden had also looked like a living, breathing human being.

At first blush, at least.

"My name is Dr. Simon Transky," the man said with a nod. "And your friend needs some serious help."

Cal internalized this information, but didn't stop his forward progress. As he neared, the doctor stepped back from Robert and the travois.

"I don't want you—" but before he could finish his sentence, Cal's legs buckled.

At first, he thought he was going to collapse on his fallen friend, crushing his motionless body, but strong arms hooked beneath his armpits and lowered him backward.

The man from the helicopter gently lowered him onto the grass before darkness once again swept over Cal.

His final thought before things went black was something that less than six months ago would have sealed his fate in an insane asylum: *Well, at least they're alive... at least they're not vengeful apparitions...*

Chapter 33

"YOU CAN CALL ME Ames," the man from the helicopter said. "Officially, I am the Director of the FBI Department of Crimes Against Children."

Cal put the two pills in his mouth—which he suspected were much stronger than Aspirin—and chased them with a mouthful of scalding coffee.

Dr. Ames... where have I heard that name before?

"And unofficially?"

The man frowned.

"We'll get to that soon enough. My colleague here," Ames said, gesturing toward the thin man with the white hair seated beside him, "Is Dr. Simon Transky."

The man smiled at the mention of his name, revealing a row of perfectly straight teeth. It was a smile that almost completely disarmed Cal.

Almost.

"Call me Si."

Cal didn't call him anything, he just stared, his eyes darting from the faces of the men to Robert on the travois resting on the table beside them.

One of the perks of being a Director in the FBI, Cal had quickly learned, was the ability to clean out a diner to host a chat, no matter where they were.

Even in somewhere as irrelevant as Mooreshead.

However, based on the way the paint was cracking and peeling near the ceiling, the smashed linoleum tiles at their feet, and the strange smell that was a mixture of backed up sewage and rancid vegetable oil, Cal wasn't convinced that they actually had to exercise any sort of authority to empty the place out.

Who in their right mind would eat here?

"I get that you're skeptical—I get that," Ames continued. "But you need to trust us."

Cal took another gulp of coffee, rolling the liquid on his tongue to prevent it from burning. It tasted much like he expected from this place, but it had been hours since his last drink.

He figured that so long as he didn't see what the coffee pot looked like, he would be able to keep it down.

"How do you know who I am? Who Robert is?" he asked, his eyes narrowing.

Ames folded his arms across his chest.

"The Cloak—"

And with that word, Cal realized why he recognized the name Ames. It was the cell phone... Brett Cherry's cell phone had rung the last time they were all together, and he had passed it to Chloe, telling her that Director Ames needed to speak to her. And hadn't Chloe said something about a helicopter?

Cal wasn't sure, but thought he might have overheard her speaking about one.

Director Ames suddenly stood and leaned over the table.

"Cal? You okay? You need—"

Cal shook him off.

"I'm fine. Why did you call Brett and Hugh away? We... we..." *needed them*, he wanted to say, but his mind was suddenly flooded with images of Chloe as she was pulled backward, rotting fingers probing her mouth and nose, the mangled orifice slowly filling with sea water.

"Fuck," he said with a shudder. He ground his teeth and turned his head to one side to try to fight back tears.

Ames's eyes narrowed.

"Where's the Cloak?" he asked softly.

Cal shook his head, but couldn't formulate a verbal response. His reaction was evidently sufficient, as Director Ames bowed his head solemnly.

Silence fell over the group, only to be broken a minute or so later by Ames.

"Hugh and Brett had to take care of something else, something important."

Cal's eyes shot up.

"What could be more important than this?" he hissed. "What could be more important than Chloe's life? Than the life of Shelly and Robert's child? *Their* lives?"

Dr. Transky leaned forward.

"I can see that you're upset, but—"

"Oh, you can, can you?" Cal turned and glared at Ames. "Jesus, where did you get this guy? He's not just a doctor, but a fucking clairvoyant, too."

Ames wasn't impressed.

"There's no time to get into the details, Cal. We all know what's at stake here."

Cal's vision went red.

"You do? Really? You know what's at stake? Like the lives of my friends, right? Do you have any friends in the field? Out there?"

Something passed in front of Ames face then, something dark that momentarily broke his calm demeanor.

Aiden… he knew Aiden.

Cal slumped back into the worn pleather booth.

Everyone makes a sacrifice, Cal. Everyone.

"Fuck," he sighed. "I'm sorry."

Ames pressed his lips together tightly.

"It's fine. But the truth is, time is almost up. I know that there is something that you need to do in town, as there is something for us to do elsewhere," Ames looked out the grease-smeared window at the sky, which had started to darken. "I don't think they'll make it through the night."

Cal gaped.

"Who won't make it?"

Director Ames didn't answer straight away. Instead, he turned to Dr. Transky first.

Cal tried to snap his fingers, but more skin just peeled away with the friction. He swallowed the nausea that followed.

"Who?"

Ames leveled his eyes at Cal.

"Shelly—Shelly and the baby."

Cal felt his heart skip a beat.

That can't be… she couldn't have been more than three months pregnant. No way the baby's coming this soon. No fucking way.

"What do you mean?"

Ames shook his head.

"No time. We need to go."

The doctor leaned in and spoke before Cal could interject.

"We'll take good care of your friend, Cal. I know this is tough to take in, especially after all you've been through, but you need to trust us."

Cal's eyes drifted to Robert's pinched expression, his tightly closed eyes.

"No," he said simply.

"Excuse me?"

Cal looked at Ames then.

"No—you're not taking him. He's staying with me."

For the second time since stepping into the diner, Director Ames's face twisted.

"We're on your side, Cal. And Robert needs—"

"What Robert needs is to be with me," Cal said flatly. "And with me, he'll stay."

They locked eyes, and eventually, Ames broke the stare and turned to the doctor.

Dr. Transky shrugged.

"It probably won't make much of a difference," he said, "Robert's in a deep coma."

Ames nodded and then stood.

"We'll help you get him outside, but then we need to go."

Cal shook his head and then flexed his raw fingers.

"No, I'll do it. You just get to where you need to be," he said with contempt.

And then, without so much as a nod or a handshake, Dr. Si Transky and FBI Director Ames left the diner.

Cal watched as they jumped into the helicopter and then, seconds later, they were airborne.

He waited until the helicopter was but a speck in the sky before letting out an exasperated, "ahhhhhhhh" and allowing himself to shake his agonizing hands.

It took him twenty minutes to slide Robert off the table, and ten more to work the travois through the narrow space between the booths and get him outside. By that time, however, whatever drugs Si had given him had started to take effect, and the pain that seemed to coat his body like a thin layer of sweat started to subside.

His eyes drifted upward, confirming that night would soon be upon them. Which night—as in the night after he had slept on the beach, or any of the night subsequent to that horrible moment—Cal had no way of knowing.

His gaze shifted to the diner next, and he was shocked to realize that he knew the place.

Not in its present, dilapidated state, surely, but back when he had been a kid.

He and Brent and Stacey had visited here to have chocolate milkshakes when they had been pre-teens.

As had Hank...

Cal shook his head, fighting the deluge of emotions that threatened to follow.

Back in Mooreshead after all this time, after I vowed never to return.

Deep down, though, despite his words, a part of Cal knew that he would come back. Only back then, he thought his return would be for Stacy, not for a strange man in the library.

Not for the man that Chloe had called the Curator. Not with all this pressure on him, pressure for him to do god only knows what.

Please, Robert, you have to wake up. I'm not cut out for this shit.

His eyes fell on Robert's face, which had once again gone flaccid.

Wake the fuck up, Robert. Please.

Chapter 34

LIKE THE DINER, MOORESHEAD Library was in dire straights. In fact, the entire city appeared to have undergone a change for the worst over the two decades or so since Cal had lived there.

Storefronts that he had once avoided when skipping school because of the housewives and homemakers that shopped there during the day had been reduced to graffiti-covered, boarded up shops.

It was sad, but Cal was also grateful.

After all, he was a haggard looking man dragging a travois upon which lay what, to the outside observer, appeared to be a corpse through the center of town.

If someone saw him, let alone stopped him, Cal would have no idea how to explain what had happened, what had brought him to this point. In fact, if he was approached at all, Cal expected that he would shortly thereafter be sporting a tight-fitting white jacket that buckled in the front sitting in the center of a room made of airbags.

And his doctor wouldn't be the charming Si Transky with his straight teeth, but a man whose life choices could have just as easily rendered him a sadistic serial killer as a doctor, sporting a needle the size of a Louisville Slugger poised at the ready. A needle that he would just be itching to inject at the mere mention of the Marrow, let alone dead people coming back to life, about gates of Hell that needed to be closed, about a book that he had written decades ago describing a network of tunnels buried deep within the earth that he had neither heard nor seen in his entire life.

The Leporidae *burrow is long and deep...*

A shudder ran through him as he made his way up the library steps, trying not to smash the back of Robert's head on each one.

Back when Cal had visited the library in his youth, it had been a deteriorating old building. Now it looked like a building that had already crumbled, leaving only a shell in its wake.

Cal reached for the large wooden door, intent on knocking loudly or calling for the man... for Seth Parsons, the Curator... but when his hand grazed the rough, rotting surface, it swung open.

The air inside the library was stale and stagnant, like a soup warmed and then left to cool in the sink. That's what it felt like to Cal: breathing in old, thin soup full of alphabet memories.

"Jesus," he muttered, pulling the collar of his shirt up to cover his nose and mouth. This didn't smell much better; he couldn't remember the last time he changed, let alone showered. Still, the familiarity of his own funk was eons better than the library air.

As the light had since faded outside, it only took a moment for Cal's eyes to adjust to the dark interior. Swatting dust motes from in front of his face, he drew in a deep breath and uttered a tentative, "Hello?"

The echo that came back at him was so loud that Cal instinctively dropped the travois and covered his ears until it passed.

After it died, but while his ears were still ringing, he turned to look at Robert with the faint hope that the sound had awoken him.

It hadn't.

Loud enough to wake the dead, he thought incomprehensibly.

Cal dragged Robert completely inside the library, then set him down again, gently this time. He tried to close the door behind him, but the hinges were oddly devoid of rust, which made it swing freely. *Too* freely. The latch was also broken, dangling uselessly from sheared metal threads. The door remained ajar, which wasn't ideal, but what choice did he have? He was simply too exhausted to lug Robert around with him anymore.

Cal turned to the interior of the library, and he scanned the space for anything familiar. The desks were still there, but the green lamps were long gone and their surfaces, once lacquered and glossy enough to fix a cowlick in, were worn and cracked.

The librarian's desk was completely missing, the rivets that had once held it in place ripped from their sockets.

Although the wooden shelves that lined the walls were still present, the ladder used to navigate along them was not.

But that wasn't the only thing that was missing.

Cal felt his heart sink.

He couldn't see a single book—the shelves were completely empty.

"No," Cal moaned. With labored steps, he made his way over to the bookshelf, leaning down as he did.

This was the spot, the place where I put my book. The one with the green cover. The one with the diagrams inside.

But there was nothing there. Deep down, he knew that this shouldn't have come as a surprise, that he should have even expected this given the state of the diner that Ames had taken him to, but it still rocked him to his core.

Coming here, to the library, to find his book, had been his only hope.

And now that that was dashed, frustration overwhelmed him.

Cal slammed his fists down on the wooden shelf in fury and swore loudly.

Regret immediately usurped exasperation, and not only because of the pain that shot up his wrists.

Whatever Dr. Transky had given him, it wasn't *just* an analgesic; his hands seemed to swirl upon impact, giving off strange colorful, red and yellow and orange puffs like a superhero in a comic book.

Cal shook his head, trying to clear it, and stood, his eyes scanning the bookshelves a final time for his volume.

Chloe couldn't be wrong… this has *to be the place… the Curator* has *to be here… my book* has *to be here.*

Only neither of those things was present.

The library, like the entire town of Mooreshead, was empty, deserted.

Cal felt his chest hitch and then the sobs came. He barely made it back to Robert's body before he collapsed in a heap on the floor.

What happened to me? What happened —

But the sound of the door opening behind him caused his head to whip around.

In from the night stepped a man dressed in dark green rags. He looked up when he saw Cal, but instead of being startled, he offered a horrible smile complete with teeth caked with dirt and grime.

"Oh, hey there. Sorry 'bout that. Was just taking a piss. What can I help you with?"

Chapter 35

"**DON'T COME NEAR US,**" Cal warned. "We don't have any-thing—no money, no drugs."

The man in the rags chuckled. It was a grating sound, one that made Cal uncomfortable. That, coupled with the fact that the man seemed to be trailing a strange yellow glow as he moved past them and deeper into the library, was enough to raise concern.

"Oh, but you want something, don't you? I mean, maybe it's knowledge... a history lesson, perhaps?" the man spoke in a slow, patronizing manner.

Cal squinted hard and with a groan, rose to his feet.

History lesson?

The words sounded oddly familiar...

"Also, this is my home. So, it's quite rude for you to shout at me when I get back from taking a piss."

Cal wasn't sure, but he thought he detected a slight hint of a Californian accent. It was difficult to tell with his teeth so caked full of shit as they were.

"Who are you?" he gasped.

The man froze.

"Ah, you know who I am, Callum Godfrey formally of this beautiful town," he replied with a chuckle.

"It can't be," Cal gasped.

The smile fell off the man's face and he strode forward so suddenly that despite everything, Cal cowered.

"What? You don't recognize me?" he asked. His breath was rank, and Cal felt his stomach lurch.

The man's hands shot up and for a second, Cal thought that he was going to throttle him. Instead, the man covered his own face with his tattered gloves. He paused, there was a bright flash of the strange yellow glow, then he pulled them away again.

The brown smile was gone. The eyes, the pale blue eyes were the same, but everything else was *different*.

"What the fuck..." Cal muttered as he staggered backward. He tripped on the corner of the travois and fell hard on his ass.

The man's face was young and smooth, and he had long blond hair that fell to his shoulders.

It was Seth Parsons.

"How did you—what did you—how—"

The man laughed, this time in a melodic timbre.

"Oh god, after all you've seen, this is what you have a hard time believing?"

Cal found himself at a loss for words.

The man's face...it had changed.

Instantly.

"Alright, how about this then? This one is going to blow your fucking mind."

Seth brought his still gloved hands in front of his face and covered it for another second.

When he pulled them away, he was once again a different person. He was fatter, with a huge, sagging chin that hung down like a peach-colored rooster waddle, and he had short black hair that was slicked against his skull.

Even though Cal had never seen this person before, something deep down told him who it was.

It was Mayor Steven Partridge.

The mayor laughed, sending his chins quivering.

"Yep, that's me, too. Steven Partridge."

Cal blinked and then tried to swallow, but his mouth felt so dry that he found himself unable.

"You... you were there? At The Pit? All those years ago?"

The man shrugged, passed his hands in front of his face, and his features seamlessly returned to those of the bum who had walked through the door moments ago. It all happened so fast that if Cal had been pressed, he might have agreed that none of the face-changing had happened, that it was all just an exhaustion- and drug-fueled hallucination.

"I've been many people during my long years in this world and others, Cal. Many different people, and not all of them were—how can I say this—model citizens."

Cal tried to swallow, but again failed. When he spoke next, his voice had a tacky quality that under other circumstances would have driven him crazy.

Except he was convinced he was already insane. Or, at the very least, extremely deranged.

"You threw McCabe in The Pit?" Cal asked. "Why?"

The man waved his question away with a gloved hand.

"That's all in the past, but if you must know—and I figure you might judging by the way your eyes are bulging out of your head—Father McCabe wasn't all that he seemed."

Seth, or whoever he was, strode toward Cal and leaned down to whisper in his ear.

"Breaking news, Callum: not all priests are good people; not all priests are of Father Callahan's quality. Besides, a sacrifice needed to be made."

He pulled away and chuckled.

Cal shook his head, trying to clear it, but this only served to make his world spin even more.

What the hell did Dr. Transky give me?

"I'm here for the book…" he managed to croak.

"Of course, you are," Seth replied, moving toward the bookshelf. He leaned down and reached for something that wasn't there. "You know, that girl Chloe... I should be getting a hold-ing fee for all the books I've stored over the years. Yours, his..."

He pressed the wood not three inches from where Cal had slammed his fists down moments ago. Something clicked and a panel slid out. Inside, a familiar book with a green cover was revealed.

"How's the old hag doing, anyway?" Seth said as he turned back to face him.

Cal averted his eyes.

"Shit," Seth whispered. "Another fucking sacrifice, huh."

Cal looked up as Seth approached, and noticed that he was shaking his head.

"I'm sorry," he offered, but Seth ignored this comment. Clearly, he was used to loss.

Cal couldn't decide if this was a good or a bad thing.

"Here," Seth said, holding the book out to him. "You're go-ing to need this."

For a moment, Cal could only stare at the paperback. He tried to reach for it, to take it, after all, this was the reason he had come back to Mooreshead, but his arms and hands simply failed to obey.

Seth pressed his lips together and then reached out and grabbed Cal's wrist and raised his hand. Then he shoved the book between his blistered fingers.

"Don't be a pussy, take the book," he whispered, the air coming out of his mouth like fumes from a toxic waste dump.

Cal squeezed the cover and was transported back to his youth, to the time when he was scribbling away in the book thinking he was under some sort of spell, under the influence of toxic mold spores, perhaps.

He shook his head then moved toward the door.

Seth chuckled.

"You forgetting something?" he asked, nudging his chin toward Robert and the travois. "Best not leave him here... besides, I think you're going to need him, too."

Cal licked his lips, trying, and failing, to moisten them. He tucked the book into the belt of his pants and leaned down to grab the travois handles.

"Yeah, that's one book that I'm not touching ever again, no matter how much—" he stopped himself before saying Chloe's name. "Anyways, good touch on the magic mushrooms, too. Those things always help, let me tell you."

Chapter 36

CAL MADE IT TO The Pit in a daze under the shroud of darkness. Seth had been right; he felt high, as if he had swallowed an entire ounce of magic mushrooms.

But he wasn't complaining. If anything, the drugs helped numb some of what he was feeling.

Unbelievably, he had made it to Mooreshead, and had acquired his book from the shape-shifting curator. And now he was here, at The Pit, waiting for…

For what? What's next, Cal? Ye of the master plan? What are you supposed to do now?

He remembered Director Ames's words, his encouragement to hurry, that Shelly and the baby wouldn't last through the night.

Cal set Robert and the travois down on the edge of The Pit, and looked around. Night was upon them, but the moon was full and bright, offering more than enough illumination for… whatever it was he was supposed to do next.

What felt like eons ago, back when he and Robert and Shelly had been living together in the Harlop Estate, he had shouted at Robert to stop acting like a boss, to stop ordering them around.

Robert had said that he was out, that he wanted none of this life, that all he wanted was to grieve the loss of his wife and daughter. But Shelly and Cal had insisted, had gone as far as to say that they would go on hunting ghosts with or without him.

Now, back at his childhood haunt, he wanted nothing more than for Robert's eyes to flick open and for the man to speak, to tell him what to do next.

Shit, he didn't care if Robert ordered him to count every grain of sand in The Pit; he'd do it.

He'd groom Wrigley Field with a pair of nail clippers, drain Lake Huron with a straw, build a life-size replica of the goddamn Great Wall of China with Play-Doe if the man would *only just wake the fuck up!*

Cal wasn't cut out for this leadership business, for being responsible for making final decisions, regardless of what Chloe had said. It was too much pressure for a man who never even completed high school.

Something in the back of his mind, however, reminded him that Robert wasn't some sort of Ivy League genius. He was a retired accountant, after all. Hell, technically, he wasn't even retired; he'd been fired.

Cal closed his eyes and shook his head.

Chloe told me to take over, that I should lead the guardians. She must know something, doesn't she?

But he was hard-pressed to put much stock in the words of a woman who had given herself up to the Goat's long dead and rotting minions.

He opened his eyes, hoping that something had appeared in front of him—a scroll, a magic bean for fuck's sake—clueing him into what to do next.

But there was only the moon above and sleeping Robert at his side.

Dejected, Cal flopped into a seated position like a petulant child. As he did, something dug painfully into his stomach and he looked down.

The book! Of course!

Cal pulled the book—*his* book—from his waistband and held it in both hands. It felt smaller than he remembered, lighter, but he couldn't be certain as his hands were still numb. The cover, previously unblemished, now bore a title and the name of the author.

He ran his fingers over the gold-embossed letters as he read the words: *The Marrow*.

And then beneath that: *Callum Godfrey*.

The letters felt so strange, both on his tongue and beneath his blistered fingers, that he had to read them a second and third time before they really started to sink in.

I wrote this, he thought absently. *I have no idea how, no clue why, but I wrote this.*

Then he pulled the cover open and started to read.

Chapter 37

THERE WEREN'T MANY WORDS in *The Marrow*. If anything, it was written more like an engineering manual than any sort of literary novel.

The book described a series of tunnels buried deep in the earth, tunnels that extended outward from the center like spokes on a wheel. And like the tire portion of a wheel, the spokes were also connected to each other in a circular fashion.

Cal read the names of the places inscribed beneath each of the spokes, some of which he knew, while others he had never heard of before.

Mooreshead, Stumphole Swamp, Askergan County, Sacred Heart.

There were more, too—nine in total by his count—but the pencil markings had faded over the years and he found himself unable to make out all the names.

Mooreshead... all these years, and there was a tunnel beneath the city. Mooreshead... the most boring town on Earth just got a little more interesting.

Cal raised his eyes and stared out over the old Forrester Gravel Pit. The place brought back horrible memories, most of which he had blocked out, but when his gaze fell on the rusted backhoe bucket, complete with red stains coating the fingers, his body clenched.

That much he recalled; no amount of therapy, denial, or time and space could make him forget what happened that night.

Hank... I'm sorry, Hank.

Cal shook his head before emotions overtook him, and he turned his attention back to the book.

It wasn't completely devoid of words, although the prose was more point-form than narrative.

On the first page, which was mostly covered with a drawing of a sterile tunnel, was a description of the tiled interior, complete with details of the thickness of the walls, the diameter of the opening. There was also a name and number at the top of the page. The name was Mooreshead and the number was four, which was circled in the upper right-hand corner.

Cal flipped the page and looked at the tunnel ascribed with the name 'Askergan County' and the number '2'.

He made a brief mental note, then continued through the pages, stopping at Sacred Heart next.

This tunnel was marked with a '6'. Just reading that name, *Sacred Heart*, made his pulse rate quicken and evoked visions of the horrible winged creature emerging from Sean's withered chest

Cal skipped further ahead, ignoring the names of places he did not know, and then stopped when he came to a drawing of a large holding tank full of some sort of liquid. Suspended inside the tank was a man, nude, with tubes coming from his nose and mouth which extended upward.

There was a name tag near the bottom, Cal saw, but the lettering was too small and too faded to make out.

And yet, for some reason, the face, even with the tubes covering the lower half, was incredibly detailed. For a moment, Cal thought the suspended man actually looked like him. He leaned in close to get a better look and sure enough, he recognized his eyes, his ears, the lines that ran from the corners of his nose to his mouth. Even his hair looked similar to the way he used to style it, in spite of being submerged in liquid.

Cal shook his head, and the image seemed to swirl before his eyes. With this came another bout of nausea.

"You're just high," he whispered out loud. "That quack Dr. Transky fed you some drugs and now you're losing it. It's not me... why would it be me?"

And yet despite his verbal admonition, he couldn't quite shake the feeling that this *was* him floating inside the tank.

Cal was about to shut the book when a pregnant drop of rain landed on the page. The liquid landed directly on the face of the person in the tank, instantly distorting his features.

Cal looked upward and squinted.

The sky was completely clear, devoid of any clouds, and the moon still shining bright.

"What the hell?"

Cal turned back to the page and saw that instead of obscuring the face, the raindrop had changed it.

I'll be damned...

Somehow, it looked like Shelly now, with her thick, red lips, her short blond hair. He was reminded briefly of how the Curator had changed his appearance, had gone from a vagrant to a surfer to a prestigious mayor from nearly a century ago simply by waving his hands in front of his face.

And then he recalled what Carson had blathered about, what at the time Cal had considered the simple ramblings of a lunatic: the self, and how giving it up meant—

Another raindrop fell, only this time it landed on Cal's nose instead of the page.

Once again, he turned his eyes upward, only this time he was met by a deluge of rain.

"Shit!" he swore, slamming the book closed and tucking it into his waistband. He pulled his grimy t-shirt over top and then went to Robert at his side, trying his best to shield him from the brunt of the downpour.

"Jesus Christ!"

In seconds, Cal was soaked through to the bone. It was as if the sky had suddenly just opened, and God Almighty had emptied a celestial bucketful right here in Mooreshead, right on The Pit, on Cal himself.

I've got to get Robert out of the rain, he thought, reaching for the travois handles.

He glanced around, hoping to find some foliage to duck under instead of having to drag the travois all the way back to what had once been Mr. Willingham's forest.

There was an outcropping of bushes to his left, he noted, and was about to start toward them when he saw something across from him, on the other side of The Pit.

A shape, a form.

And then a voice filtered to him over the quarry. A voice that made his heart stop cold.

"Cal? Is that you, Cal?"

Cal dropped the travois.

Chapter 38

"IT'S COMING ANYTIME NOW."

Shelly's eyes rolled back in her head and she moaned, feeling the pressure inside her build to new heights.

Oh, the baby was coming alright, but it wasn't coming out of her vagina. It felt as if it was going to tear its way out of her stomach.

"And when it comes? What then?" a different voice asked.

Shelly allowed her head to roll in that direction, and through half-open and fluttering lids, she made out a familiar face.

It was the face of Carson Black, and the bastard was smiling.

"Then we bind the child of two guardians to the living and the dead. We open the gates."

Shelly saw Carson nod in her periphery.

"And what about Bella and the orphans? What if they're not back in time?"

There was a sudden crunch inside her, somewhere in the general vicinity of her belly button, and Shelly shrieked.

"Get it out!" she screamed. "*Get it out!*"

A dry chuckle filled the room.

"Oh, it'll come out, sweetie, but you can't rush these things."

For several agonizing minutes, the only sound in the room was Shelly's own staggered breathing. And then Carson repeated his question.

"What about Bella and the orphans?"

"They're gone, Carson. They served us well, but now they're gone. As is Robert—I thought we could change him, make him come to his senses, but, alas, he always was a mama's boy."

This was followed by dry laughter.

"It's just me and you dad, just like it's always been."

Robert… he's gone?

Something inside Shelly snapped like a guy-wire under tension, and this time she couldn't even scream.

This time, her entire body tensed, including her heart and lungs, crippling her.

The baby's coming! Oh god, the baby's coming right now!

Chapter 39

"YOU CAME BACK!"

Cal stared over The Pit.

It can't be.

But it *could* be, he knew this deep down. He had seen the dead return, had seen them walking the earth with his own eyes. For the most part, however, these apparitions had been strangers, people with families and lives, surely but not his family, not his life.

Never had someone he known and loved returned from the dead and even though he knew it possible, his damaged mind couldn't wrap itself around the idea.

"It's not real... it's not real... it's not real," he repeated over and over even as the figure started to walk along the edge of The Pit toward him.

Cal covered his ears with his hands and closed his eyes. Then he started to rock back and forth.

It's the rain and the drugs. It's the exhaustion and the stress messing with me... it can't be real.

The rain continued to beat down on him, but when he heard no other sound, no mention of his name, Cal stopped rocking and opened his eyes.

Not ten paces to his left stood his childhood friend Hank, his beanpole frame stooped, hands jammed into the pocket of his jeans. Unlike the children from the orphanage, he looked exactly the way he had on the day he died.

Cal wasn't sure if this made it easier or harder to believe.

"Hank?" he whispered. The rain on his face mixed with his tears, fully soaking him now. "Is that really you?"

Hank shrugged and smiled, revealing his large teeth.

"In the flesh, Cally-boy. In the flesh."

Cal just stared, finding himself unable to move, to speak.

How can this be? I saw him die… saw him pulled under the water by the hands.

Hank looked away from him then, and peered down into The Pit.

Water had started to build at the bottom, and while it was still relatively calm, Cal knew that it was only a matter of time before it started to churn and froth.

And the hands… the hands will return.

"I ever tell you about the history of the Forrester Gravel Pit?" Hank asked, his back still turned. There was something wrong with his spine, Cal realized. It was hard to tell exactly what because of the downpour, but it didn't seem straight. "About the Mayor and the Priest?"

There was also a dark maroon spot between his shoulder blades. It took Cal a few moments to realize that Hank wasn't stooped as he had first thought.

The boy's back had been shattered from when Cal had pushed him off the ledge and he had struck the backhoe.

Hank turned.

"I know, I know, it sounds like a bad joke, but there really is a deep, rich history to Mooreshead."

Cal didn't say anything; he only wept silently.

Does he even know he's dead?

"No? Not interested? Well, how about this one? How about the one about the boy who pushed his best friend into The Pit, hmm? About how he was so jealous of his friend getting the girl that he just out and killed him? Fucking *murdered* his best friend. How 'bout that one?"

Cal's eyes widened as Hank strode toward him.

So much for not remembering what happened.

The boy's lips pulled back from his teeth, revealing a sinister grin. Only then did Cal notice that Hal's eyes were black as coal.

"You killed me, Cal. You were my best friend—I loved you—and you *killed* me," he hissed.

Cal shuddered and stepped backward.

"I'm sorry!" he shouted. "I'm so fucking sorry! I didn't mean to do it!"

Hank continued to walk toward him in large, loping strides that quickly closed the distance between them.

"You thought Mooreshead was boring, huh? So, what, you decided to make your own excitement? What were you thinking? Fuck Hank, nobody likes the scrawny, pimply bastard anyway. I'll kill him, make a story for myself. Then I'll run away like a coward. Does that pretty much sum it up?"

Cal shook his head violently from side to side.

"No! I didn't mean to! It was an accident!"

Hank turned his face up to the rain and laughed. He sputtered, coughed, then leveled his black eyes at Cal.

No longer was his face youthful, vibrant. Like the Curator, Hank's visage had changed.

Only his friend didn't become a good-looking surfer with long blond hair and pale blue eyes. Instead, he became something... *horrible*. Something dead.

Mud and dirt clung to his nostrils in thick clumps, caked his swollen eyelids, and made dirty tracks down the sides of his face like tanned arteries. Maggots wriggled at the corners of his lips like tiny, white tongues.

"You killed me," Hank hissed. Something like a hiccup passed through his body, and moments later several thin, black legs pushed back his rotting lips. Cal watched in horror as the entire, two-inch carapace of a carrion beetle emerged from his friend's mouth. The beetle's beady black eyes, not unlike

Hank's own, stared at Cal as it scrambled onto the boy's cheek where it rested. "You killed me, and now I'm going to kill you!"

And then Hank lunged.

Cal barely managed to sidestep Hank's grasp. The boy's hands passed within inches of his face, before he stumbled by him, almost toppling on top of Robert in the process.

"Please," Cal pleaded as Hank threw his head back, spraying wet hair from his face. His spine made an awful grating sound as he did this, and when he extricated his body from the mud, it didn't look quite right.

Hank's backbone didn't line up properly.

"This your friend, Cal?" Hank said as he shambled back toward him.

At first, Cal wasn't sure what he was talking about and he shook his head.

"What are—"

But then he realized that Hank mustn't have seen Robert until now, what with the rain coming down as it was, and the fact that he was lying on the dark travois of to one side.

"Don't even think about it," Cal said, his voice suddenly hardening. "Get away from him."

Hank laughed again and the beetle on his cheek reared up as if posing for its own, separate attack.

"Oh, this is your new best friend, now? Is that it? You going to kill him, too?" Hank took two steps forward. "I'll tell you what; I'll spare you the trouble and do it myself."

Hank leaned down toward Robert's sleeping face, and Cal immediately sprang to action.

"No!" he screamed.

Seth Parson's words—not from this day, but from a long time ago—echoed in his head.

You will one day make your sacrifice as well, Cal.

And in that moment, Cal was certain that this is what the shape-shifting curator had meant. He would sacrifice himself in this moment, bind himself to Hank, so that Robert could rise from his coma and end all this.

Cal was never meant to lead.

Cal was meant to suffer.

"*Stop!*" another voice rang out from behind them.

Cal paused mid-lunge and turned.

And in that moment, he realized that he was wrong.

Chapter 40

"STACEY?" HANK AND CAL said in unison.

Stacy stepped out of the shadows and approached. Her face was exactly as Cal remembered it; he could never forget the face of the girl he had lusted after for so long.

The girl who Hank had taken from him, taken for his own by tricking him.

"Where... where did you come from?" Cal stammered.

Stacey looked at him, sneered, then turned to Hank.

"What happened to you... Hank, that was an accident. A stupid, freak accident."

Hank's face contorted.

"It wasn't an accident. Cal pushed me... he wanted me to die. He murdered me."

Cal sidled quietly toward the travois and hooked a foot behind one of the makeshift handles.

"I didn't want you to die!" he yelled. "You were my best fucking friend. But you... you slept with Stacey even though you knew I loved her!"

Hank recoiled as if he had been struck, but Stacey was the one who answered.

"I'm nobody's property, Cal, I told you that before. You don't own me—neither of you do."

Cal blinked hard, clearing the rain from his eyes.

The conversation was strange and had an air of déjà vu even though it was slightly off.

Something's not right.

"But... but... he pushed me!" Hank accused, leveling a decomposing finger at Cal's chest.

Cal nodded as he nudged the travois a foot or so toward the edge of The Pit.

He knew now what he had to do, what his sacrifice was, and it wasn't to bind himself to his dead friend.

His sacrifice was to let go. To just... *let go.*

"I pushed you," Cal admitted, eyes downcast. "And I've lived my entire life regretting that decision each and every day. There's nothing I can say or do to make it better, to change what happened. I can only tell you how I feel."

When the only answer was a splinter of lightning, followed quickly by a rumble of thunder, he raised his eyes.

Only he didn't look directly at his friends. Instead, he turned to The Pit. The water had started to bubble at the bottom like a pond filled with thousand of feeding minnows.

Not much time... I don't have much time before they come again. And when they do, it'll all be over. I won't be able to access the tunnel, enter Marrow 4.

His eyes skipped from Hank's to Stacey's and back again.

"How do you feel?" Stacey whispered.

Cal took a deep breath.

"I feel like a piece of shit. Truly, I feel like a hot, steaming turd. I never meant to hurt anyone, let alone you two, my best friends. I just wanted... something more," he shrugged. "I know how that sounds, I do, but it's the truth. And I'm more sorry about what happened than you can ever imagine."

Stacey nodded in silent acceptance, but Hank was having none of it.

"You can't change the facts, Cally-boy. You killed me, and for two decades I've been waiting to return the favor. Now —"

He reached for Cal mid-sentence, catching him off guard. Hank's arms were spread wide in a massive embrace, and when Cal tried to move, his feet stuck in the mud.

This is it... my time is up. I'm sorry, Robert. I'm sorry, Chloe and Shelly and Aiden. I've let you all down.

But an instant before the dead hands reached him, Stacey moved between them, her own arms open almost comically wide. She encompassed Hank with the largest hug imaginable, one that Cal so wanted to give but couldn't.

"No!" Cal screamed, but it was too late. Stacey's body immediately bucked and started to shimmer. "No, Stacey! What have you done?"

Stacey flicked her head around and looked at him.

"Go now, Cal. Your sacrifice has been made. The *Leporidae* burrow is long and deep, but it's also going to get a whole lot more crowded the longer you wait."

Realization washed over Cal.

This wasn't Stacey—after all, Stacey would be in her midthirties now, while this girl, the one that Hank was now kissing hungrily with his decomposing lips, was only fifteen.

The Leporidae burrow *is long and deep...*

Cal didn't hesitate. He flicked his foot, spinning Robert's travois around and then pushed.

It skittered then started down the slope of the quarry like a runaway toboggan.

"Thank you," Cal whispered back at the Curator. "And I'm sorry, Hank. I really, truly am."

Then he jumped headlong into The Pit.

Chapter 41

THE MUD WAS SLICKER than Cal remembered from all those years ago, and as a result, he slid much faster than Hank had the night he died. Halfway down, he had to angle his sore body to one side to avoid braining himself on the backhoe that had taken his friend's life.

But while Cal's descent was fast, Robert's was like a marble shot over ice. The travois *flew* down the side of The Pit with lightning speed.

"*Fucking heeeeeeelllllllll!*"

Robert hit the water first, and his travois skipped over the surface, before banging roughly against the opposing incline. The belt that Cal had used to fasten his legs to the wood must have slipped during the descent, as Robert's unconscious body started to slide off the travois.

Cal splashed down, taking in a huge mouthful of the strangely salty water. He sputtered, spat, and then half-waded half-swam over to his friend, grabbing him by the shoulders just before he became completely submerged. With a grunt, he forced Robert back onto the dark fabric before cinching the belt tight.

Then he peered around.

Cal wasn't sure what he had expected to find at the bottom of the quarry, but all told, the result was anti-climactic. His mind drifted to thoughts of the hands that had once reached up from the depths, the hands of the workers that Mayor Partridge had condemned to die, and he felt his frustration mount.

There has to be something… a door, a gateway, anything. There just has to be!

Cal looked around desperately, but he saw nothing but bubbling water all around him and rain pouring down the sides of the embankment. Just as he was about to give up hope, he spotted a part of another archaic digging machine jutting from the side of The Pit, and he tried to move toward it.

Except he couldn't; his feet were stuck. He grunted and tried to yank his worn runners, but this only made the mud suction even tighter to his ankles.

"What the fuck?"

Cal reached for the travois and grabbed hold of it, trying to use it to haul himself from the mud.

It only made things worse.

Before he had fully comprehended what was happening, the mud had reached Cal's knees.

It was futile; every movement just caused him to sink even deeper.

Cal decided that he had no other choice. With a silent prayer to a god he didn't believe in, he grabbed the travois with both hands and then drove his heels downward as hard as he could.

There was an audible *slurp* and before he knew it, the mud was up to mid-thigh. But the strange thing was, he found he could move his feet freely, as if the mud was only a thin layer and below that…

Cal pushed again, and a second later, he found himself falling. He adjusted his hands on the travois handles one final time and shouted, "Hold on, Sleeping Beauty, we're going down!"

Chapter 42

THE FALL LASTED ONLY seconds before Cal collapsed to the hard ground. His ankle twisted awkwardly beneath him, but he felt no associated flare of pain. Whether it was sheer exhaustion, the effects of the drugs that Dr. Transky had given him, or something else entirely, he had no idea.

Nor did he care.

His hands were still extended upward, his fingers wrapped tentatively around the travois handles, but Robert was still in The Pit above or worse, submerged under the water.

For a moment, the strangeness of the ceiling caused Cal to pause: he could see a layer of wet dirt that just shouldn't be there, shouldn't be staying in place the way it was. Like him, it should have fallen.

It was like some sort of strange *Upside-Down* that made his mind swim.

A liquid gurgle drew him back to the present, and he shook his head. Then he pulled with all his might.

Robert *et al* came flying out of the sand and Cal barely managed to get out of the way. It smashed hard against the floor, bounced once, but while his friend's eyelids fluttered, they didn't open. At least he was still breathing.

"Jesus fuck, why don't you just wake up!" Cal shouted. His voice echoed up and down the hallway, the walls of which were covered in white subway tiles, just as they had been in his diagrams. In Cal's book, however, the distance between the different stops along the tunnels was short, with each of the nine locations but a stone's throw of each other. But here, inside the actual tunnel, the scale was off.

Way off.

As far as he could see in either direction, there was only more of the damn tiles.

Cal stood, and his injured ankle nearly buckled.

"Which way? Which fucking way?"

He tried to remember from the diagrams if he should head east or west to head toward Sacred Heart—for as much as he feared the place, he just knew this is where he had to return— but nothing made sense to him.

Which way is West in the Upside-Down?

Cal felt his frustration start to mount and was about to shout when the lights in the tunnel suddenly flickered. Something that Robert had said long ago occurred to him then.

The dead… they come when the lights flicker…

"Time's up," he said, bending to grab the travois handles. They felt almost natural in his hands now, an extension of himself, given how long he had been holding the damn things.

"If we ever make it out of this, Robert, I swear to God—"

But the sound of footsteps stole the words from his mouth.

Cal turned to his right, then to his left. Although he couldn't identify where the sound had come from, he saw that the tiles weren't as perfect as he had first thought: there appeared to be words scrawled on some of them. Moving quickly, he sprinted to the wall with Robert in tow.

Marrow 4, the words read. Then, beneath those were two arrows, one leading to the left marked with *Marrow 6*, while the other pointed to the right, *Marrow 2*.

Cal racked his brain, trying to remember which number was ascribed to Sacred Heart.

"Two is… Jesus, which one is two, again?" Cal reached into his belt and pulled out the book, but when he flipped open the first page, he noticed that the water at the bottom of The Pit had caused all the images to smudge.

"Fuck!" he swore, tossing it to the ground. It landed with a bang, which was quickly followed by an inhuman growl from somewhere deep in the catacombs.

Cal clenched his teeth.

I'm running out of time! They're coming! What was the name of the strange place again, the—

"Askergan County was number 2!" he exclaimed. He pumped a fist, then made a conscious decision to head away from Marrow 2 and toward Marrow 6. He wasn't sure if this was the way toward Sacred Heart, if Sacred Heart was number 6, but he was out of options.

Cal started in that direction, fueled by more of the guttural snarls that seemed to grow louder as he walked.

He hadn't made it more than twenty paces before a doorway suddenly appeared at his right, and Cal peered inside.

The room was filled with huge tanks that extended nearly to the ceiling. Inside the first tank of several was a man, nude save a mask over his nose and mouth, suspended in the liquid.

Cal knew that he had to keep moving, but there was such an uncanny, almost photographic similarity to his own drawings, that he was hypnotized by the sight.

The face... is it...

Cal had to find out if it was *him* inside the tank, as bizarre as the idea sounded. He strode forward and squinted hard.

He had black hair, and a smooth, round face. His—

The man's eyes suddenly opened wide, revealing midnight black orbs and Cal stumbled backward. His heel caught on the travois, and he fell hard on his ass.

It wasn't him, he realized, but one of the men from The Pit. Cal didn't know how he knew this, he just did. His relief, however, at the fact that he wasn't somehow transposed in two places at once, was short-lived.

As he scrambled to his feet, there was an audible hiss, and the front of the tank, a massive section of curved glass, started to cantilever forward. Water bubbled and spilled from the seams, and the man, previously still aside from his wide eyes, started to twitch and squirm.

Cal didn't need to see anymore; as the lights flickered and dimmed, he grabbed the travois handles and started to run toward *Marrow 6*, hoping that they weren't too late.

Praying that Shelly and Robert's baby hadn't been born yet.

Chapter 43

Time puckered. That was the only way Cal could describe what happened next. As he ran, dragging Robert behind him, time *puckered*.

As did distance.

Within minutes, Cal heard familiar voices echoing toward him.

Chapter 44

SHELLY SCREAMED.

"It's coming! Get it out!"

The room was spinning, and she felt on the verge of losing consciousness before a hand slapped her hard across the face.

"Oh, no you don't," Carson whispered. "You're going to stay awake for this. You *need* to stay awake."

Shelly didn't care about anything but getting the child out of her. The pain was like nothing she had ever experienced before, nor ever wanted to come close to experiencing again.

Her belly tightened, and this time she went with the contraction, squeezing as hard as she possibly could.

There was a tearing sound, and then, finally, some relief in the form of pressure release. She felt more of the sticky liquid coat her lower half, but she couldn't bear to look.

"The head!" Carson exclaimed, "I can see the head!"

A wave of tension came again, and Shelly shrieked once more. She pushed and felt both of her legs go completely numb as something big started to crawl out of her.

"Stop!" a voice shouted and at first, she thought it was Carson, or maybe Leland. But when the command came a second time, she realized it was neither. It was Cal's voice, and at long last, Shelly gained the courage to open her eyes.

Chapter 45

"STOP!" CAL SHOUTED AS he stepped into *Marrow 6*, the room located directly below Sacred Heart Orphanage.

He thought he issued the order again, but was too overcome by the horrifying sight before him to be sure.

Shelly was naked, splayed on a metal gurney like an anesthetized sow prepared for slaughter. Her legs, wrists, and neck were bound with twine, and her upper half was covered in a sheen of sweat.

But this paled in comparison to the mess from the waist down.

Blood was everywhere—thick, dark splotches of congealed blood stained her legs, the gurney, while fresh red smears coated the underside of her burgeoning belly.

And she was crowning, good God if she wasn't *crowning* before his eyes.

Cal could see the top of a baby's head starting to protrude from between her legs, a crop of matted black hair clinging to the deformed scalp.

Carson was standing by Shelly's head whispering something in her ear, smiling broadly.

Leland, dressed in his patented faded jean jacket, his black hat pulled low and hiding his face, stood against the back wall, his arms crossed over his chest.

"Glad you can make it, Cal. You've arrived just in time," Leland said calmly.

"Stop!" Cal repeated, but this time the word came out as a whimper.

But when Shelly screamed again, he realized that his words were futile. Leland must have come to the same conclusion as he started to laugh.

Shelly had reached the point of no return.

"Too late, Cally-boy. You're too late. The baby's here."

And then, with one final shriek that nearly burst Cal's eardrums, the baby gushed forth in a geyser of fluid.

Shelly went silent, as did everyone else in the room. Except, of course, for the crying newborn.

Chapter 46

TOO LATE... YOU'RE TOO late...

After all, it had taken to get here, after all, he had been through, Cal was still too late to put a stop to the inevitable.

Shelly and Robert's baby was born, and now it was only a matter of minutes before *they* took the child and bound it to the living and the dead. And then the gates of Hell would open, and quiddity from the Marrow would be able to flow back into this world.

There was only one thing that Cal could think of to do, one final, desperate play to put a stop to this horror.

"Give me the baby," he hissed.

Carson was cradling the child now, cooing at its blood covered face, all the while the cord was still attached to its belly button and the placenta buried deep inside Shelly.

Leland pushed himself away from the wall.

"Yeah, good luck with that."

As he spoke, the Goat tilted his head back slightly, revealing hundreds of tiny, pointed teeth that reflected the incandescent lighting above like razor blades under moonlight.

Cal felt fear course through him, but he thought he still had time. After all, they still needed to kill someone to fulfill the triumvirate. But when Leland laughed, a dry cackle like crumbling driftwood, Cal realized that he had again made a fatal error.

The bastard was going to do it himself—Leland was going to act as the dead as, technically, he had died long ago at the hands of Sean Sommers.

"Give me the child, Carson. You hold one arm, and I'll hold the other. Let's open the gates, son. Let's finish this."

Carson nodded, and stepped around the gurney, cradling the crying child tightly in his arms.

Cal's heart sunk. Even if he managed to get to Carson and somehow subdue him, that would still leave Shelly and himself as possible living components of the Holy Trinity.

"I'm too late," he whispered, to which Leland responded with another grating laugh.

"Finally! After all these years," Leland exclaimed as he reached up and grabbed the brim of his black hat between two talons. "After all—"

"I'll take it from here, Cal," a voice from behind him suddenly interrupted. "This is, after all, a family matter."

Chapter 47

ROBERT IGNORED THE SHOCK on Cal's face and after briefly surveying the scene, he confirmed his decision. He had come to the moment that Cal had pulled him into the room, into *Marrow 6*, and while playing possum, he had weighed his options.

There was only one move that made sense to him, only one act that could save the world, at least for the time being.

Robert just hoped that Cal knew what to do after he had played his role, but given that his friend had brought him this far, he had little doubt.

It was Cal's show now, and he was absolutely, unequivocally okay with that. For all his shortcomings, Cal was a good, honest man.

And the world would do well with him in charge of protecting the living from the dead.

"Robert! Robert, you're... *awake!*" Cal exclaimed.

Robert nodded briskly and strode forward.

"Ah, son, I'm so glad that you're here to see this. I'm so glad that we're together again!"

Robert turned to Carson, who was gently tickling the baby's blood and vernix covered chin.

"Welcome back, brother," he said with a grin.

Leland yanked the hat off his head and threw it to the floor and Robert instinctively cringed.

Chloe Black's face had been mangled, scarred, deformed, but it had at least been recognizably human. Leland on the other hand... the man's face was one of pure blackness, like oil at night, broken only by thousands of tiny pointed teeth that ran the width of his demonic grin.

In the place of eyes were two glowing red pits.

The sight of the Goat's face was so horrible, so *evil*, that Robert nearly reconsidered his decision.

But he didn't.

It was his turn to make the ultimate sacrifice.

He lunged not at the baby as both Carson and Leland, and perhaps Cal, expected but at Leland himself.

For Leland was the dead third of the Trinity, and if he could reach him, if Robert could just graze his dead flesh, they would both be sent back to the Marrow. Because despite what his father said, he meant something to the man, and should he just make contact they would be intrinsically bound, the way James Harlop had been bound to the wrought iron poker that he had used to brain his wife and Dr. Andrew Shaw had been bound to his notebook.

"No!" Leland roared, finally realizing what Robert was intending to do. But his understanding came too late.

I'm coming, Amy! I'm coming!

Robert didn't want to look at his baby, given that he had lost one already, but he couldn't help it. As his body, launched like a projectile, passed his brother, he turned his head and laid his eyes on his child for the first and only time.

It was a girl, he realized. A beautiful, perfect baby girl.

I love you, Shelly, he managed to think just before he made contact with Leland. *Please, look after our child.*

"No!" Leland roared again.

Yes, Robert thought as tears spilled from his eyes. *Yes.*

Arms outstretched, he grabbed his father.

Only he never touched him.

Just before they made contact, Robert felt something inside him break.

Chapter 48

NOW, HELEN! I NEED you now! Come forward! Take over Robert's body now!

Chapter 49

CAL WATCHED THE SCENE unfold before him with morbid fascination.

It wasn't him who had to make the ultimate sacrifice, he realized, but Robert. He knew that now, much like he knew that he was going to grab the baby from Carson even before the man dropped it.

And yet while he managed to catch the baby before it struck the gurney, the other part of the equation—Robert's sacrifice—simply failed to materialize.

Cal heard Leland shout, but this quickly transitioned into a laugh.

Shelly grunted and delivered the placenta, and Cal, using the distraction to his advantage, stepped forward and with his free hand reached beneath the table. Her bindings were connected by a central tether, and with one yank, he managed to snap her free.

He looked over and saw that Leland was indeed hugging Robert, but when he caught sight of his friend's eyes, they were completely back.

Helen, he thought miserably. *Helen had come forth.*

He had seen her do this once before, in the orphanage above. Robert couldn't bind to Leland when Helen was in charge of his body, because she, like the Goat, was dead.

How long she could maintain her hold, however, Cal wasn't sure. But he knew it wouldn't be long.

With the baby cradled in one arm, he leaned over and reached behind Shelly's head. In one swift motion, he managed to hoist her to a sitting position. Her eyes rolled forward, and she seemed to awaken.

"What's happening?" she whispered.

Cal shifted her off the gurney and was surprised that despite the blood loss and having just delivered a child, that she was able to shuffle with him.

Her eyes fell on the wailing baby in Cal's arm.

"Is that... is that my child?" she sobbed.

Cal nodded as he lowered her onto travois. Then he pressed the newborn against her bare chest.

The black fabric that made up the base of the travois was longer on one side, and he flipped it over Shelly and her baby. For a second, it covered her face, and he was reminded of Chloe and the cloak she used to wear.

Before running from the room, Cal turned back one final time to say goodbye to his friend.

Leland was still holding Robert, but now Carson had embraced them as well. Robert's eyes started to lighten as Helen descended back into the depths of his mind. When they went completely clear, Cal heard Leland's laughter again.

Then he turned and fled *Marrow 6*.

Robert, like the baby clasped in Shelly's arms, was also a child of two guardians and sandwiched between the Goat and Carson, the Holy Trinity was complete.

Cal was partway down the white hallway when everything was suddenly bathed in an impossibly bright light.

And then the gates to Hell opened.

Chapter 50

WHEN THE LIGHTS FLICKERED, Director Ames turned his eyes skyward, his lips pressed together into a scowl.

They stabilized and he lowered his gaze to the man performing the operation.

Dr. Simon Transky stood with a scalpel poised over Landon Underhill's exposed brain, a look of confusion on his face. He lowered the scalpel, but then pulled back before making contact. He repeated this action several times before shaking his head and stepping away from the operating table.

He placed the scalpel in the plastic kidney shaped dish and then pulled the mask from his face with a gloved hand.

"Ames? I see both enlarged anterior and posterior cingulate cortexes, and also—"

An eruption of light, as if a flashbang grenade had been tossed inside the operating room stunned Ames and he staggered. The only thing that prevented him from going down was the large oak desk to his right.

"Si! Si! Get down! They failed!" he shouted, gripping the sides of the desk as the ground beneath his feet began to quake. "They *fucking* failed!"

Epilogue

AMY WATTS TURNED HER eyes upward just as the sky above started to hiss and burn. She had seen this before, of course. She had seen it each and every time that her grandfather came to visit.

But it had been a while since Leland had taken her on the boat to the island and left her there. He promised that he would return, that he would come back for her, but she was beginning to have her doubts.

She liked her grandpa. Not as much as daddy—oh, how she missed daddy—but grandpa was nice to her. Which was why when the sky erupted into flames, instead of being scared as she normally was—the faces in the flames were frightening, what with them screaming all the time, screaming and yelling and changing—she was a tad excited.

Amy looked down and stroked the miniature turtle in her hand. The creature craned its neck and looked up at her and then it seemed to nod.

"Grandpa's coming," Amy said quietly.

The turtle blinked.

There was a crack, like dry lightning, and Amy turned her gaze skyward once more.

Her heart sunk.

Grandpa wasn't coming.

No one was.

In fact, everyone was leaving.

There was a hole in the sky, a giant gaping chasm that started to swirl, rippling along the edges like the eye of a tornado.

And then the faces, the faces that scared Amy so much that she hadn't slept in what seemed like forever, started to form in the fire, only to be swept up into the vortex and whisked away.

With a sigh, she turned her gaze back to the turtle in her palm. It was looking up at her with gold-rimmed eyes.

"No, he's not coming," Amy Watts said, fighting back tears. "No one's coming for us. No one."

END

Author's Note

Robert tried.

Cal tried

Shelly most definitely tried. And in their own way, so did Chloe and Aiden.

This is not the end of the journey for The Haunted Series family, not in the least. But it is the end of the first arc of the story.

In its essence, The Haunted Series is a journey of a man and his friends coming to terms with who they are, and the difficult decisions they have to make as they transition from being normal individuals into something more. It's also about the idea of the self and what it means to be *you* and how important that is to your life.

Ah, shit, who am I kidding? It's also about ghosts and demons and the devil and hell and all that good stuff. I'm not going to lie... it's a whole lotta fun writing about Rob and his gang, about their often botched adventures.

I hope you've enjoyed these exploits, because I have. One year and six books later... it's been an exciting ride. There's plenty of more in this world to explore, including Ed and Allan's adventures in the Marrow and, of course, the consequences of Robert's actions at the end of the book.

Check back soon for more books in the series. And, as always, if you've got a comment, suggestion, or just want to chat, hit me up on my Facebook page or drop me an email.

You keep reading and I'll keep writing.

Patrick
Montreal, 2017

Made in the USA
Coppell, TX
12 December 2023

25760820R00135